THE FINGER

BY
SUSAN L. PARÉ

THE FINGER BY SUSAN L. PARÉ

THE FINGER BY SUSAN L. PARÉ

THE FINGER BY SUSAN L. PARÉ

MORE BY THIS AUTHOR

The Twisted Tree Triangle

The Box House

The Proof Is In the Pudding

Blueberries and Bears and My Brother's Shoes

Red, White, and Blue (A Short Story)

She Never Stopped Talking

Red

The House on Ludington Street

What's Behind the Screen Door?

The Mayor's Son

Willerton Woods

Floating Face Down
A Sheriff "Cowboy" Berkson Mystery Novel – Three

Let's Play Autopsy

A Bad Week In Hollister
A Sheriff "Cowboy" Berkson Mystery Novel – Two

Don't Smother Your Mother
A Sheriff "Cowboy" Berkson Mystery Novel – One

Crossing Sydney

THE FINGER BY SUSAN L. PARÉ

Index

Thank you, Pierre

I'm proud to dedicate this book to Pierre Paré, a man of many talents, a wordsmith (he once owned a book store), and good looks. (He is a Paré, after all.)

I did not know of Pierre before the fall of 2018. In fact, I didn't know any of my relatives on my father's side. My grandparents passed away when my dad was a young child and he was raised by foster parents.

I was excited when Pierre sent me an email, informing me that we were related. I responded, thrilled to know that I had a Paré relative. Did I say <u>a</u> relative? I found out that I have hundreds. Isn't DNA just something else?

Pierre told me that he had spent many years putting together a family tree. Thanks to all of his hard work, Pierre has gifted me with pictures and stories of relatives who came before and after me. Even today he works tirelessly to update the Paré family tree as he gathers more information.

Pierre is my second cousin. He lives in Montreal and the chance of us ever meeting in person is slim at this point in my life. However, we've gotten to know each other – due to gobs of emails – and I couldn't feel closer to him if we lived next door to each other.

I want to thank Pierre for taking time out of his busy days to give me his comments, suggestions, and encouragement as I shared my writing of this book with him. It has been interesting to find a person who has the same type of humor as myself. We're a rare breed. There is no doubt we are definitely related.

Thanks, Pierre. Because of you, *The Finger* has been the most fun book I have written to date. Some of your comments made me laugh, and some made me wonder if my grandchildren might just, as you jokingly asked, be afraid of me. Nah – they're not.

I wish I had known you earlier in my life. What fun we would have had.

Susan

THE FINGER

THE FINGER BY SUSAN L. PARÉ

CHAPTER ONE

<u>Monday, October 31st, Halloween Eve</u>

"For God's sake, will you help a little?" she whispered angrily.

"I am helping."

"Let's change positions. You take his legs."

"He's heavy."

"Of course, he's heavy. He was a fat pig." Fran took a deep breath, waited a moment, grabbed the man under his arms, and tried to lift him. She jumped, frightened as the doorbell rang. "Shit," she muttered under her breath.

"Are you going to answer the door?"

"You're kidding."

"Well, the lights are on. People must know we're at home," Phoebe replied.

"And, maybe we should ask a few of those trick-and-treaters to come in and help us, you twit."

"Don't call me a twit. You're the twit. This is all your fault."

"Come here and grab an arm. Maybe we can move him if we both pull on his arms."

"Do you think it would be easier if we put a rug under him? We could slide him rather than try to lift him."

"Good idea, Pheebs. You're using your brain for a change."

1

"What about the stairs?"

"What about them?"

"How are we gonna get him down the stairs?"

"One big shove and let him roll down. Damn that doorbell. Go down and turn off all the lights." She sat on the top step and waited for Phoebe to turn the lights off. "We have a problem," Fran stated when Phoebe started coming up the stairs.

"You think?"

"Even if we get him down the stairs, we still aren't going to be able to get him in the car. We're just not strong enough."

"Well, what the hell are we going to do with him?" Phoebe asked, tears welling up in her eyes.

"What? You're gonna have a breakdown now? Pull yourself together, will you?"

"This is all your fault, you know."

"There's only one thing we can do. Let's pull him into the bathroom."

"Why? It took us forever to get him this far and now you want to take him to the bathroom?"

"You were right. Let's get a rug under him. It will be easier that way."

"What are you going to do?" Phoebe asked.

"Stop asking so many questions and go get that damn throw rug out of your bedroom," Fran demanded.

"I don't know ..."

"Will you quit arguing with me and just do it, for God's sake."

"It was a lot easier moving him with the rug. That hardly took any time at all. I'll be right back," Fran declared, as she walked out of the bathroom.

"Where are you going?"

"To get a saw and some plastic bags."

Phoebe stared at her and shook her head. "No, no, no. We can't do that. I can't do that."

"It's the only way we're going to get him out of the house."

"I can't."

"You can and you will. Now, get his clothes off. I'll be right back."

"You're crazy, you know that? How can you even think about doing that?"

"Would you rather spend the rest of your life in jail?" Fran asked.

"But it was an accident. You know that. Why don't we just call the police and explain to them what happened?"

"Would you believe it? I certainly wouldn't."

"I need to think." Phoebe walked over to the stairs, sat down on the top step, and sighed. "Say we do cut him up and bag him. Just think of all of the blood that we are going to have to clean up. We'll never get it all, you know. Forensics always finds some hidden in a crack somewhere."

"Bleach will clean it up. We just have to be sure we do every surface. It would be nice if we could get him in the tub to take him apart but that's out of the question." She thought for a moment. "We need to put some plastic under him before we do it. He's dead so there shouldn't be a lot of blood," she declared.

"How do you know that?"

"I read a lot. Now take his clothes off. I'll be right back," Fran said.

"Wait. I'm coming with you."

"What in the world for?"

"I'm hungry. I want a sandwich."

"You're kidding. He's lying there dead and you want to eat?" she asked, totally astonished.

"I don't do well on an empty stomach. You know that," Phoebe replied.

"All right. Just hurry it up. I'd like to be done with this before it gets light outside."

"It's only nine o'clock. We'll be done long before that."

"Will we? Well, tell me, miss smarty pants, how many bodies have you dismembered?" She gave Phoebe a dirty look. "Well?"

"None," she mumbled.

"Damn right, none. It takes a long time to cut through those bones. We'll be lucky if we have him bagged before lunch tomorrow."

"What? No! You're joking. It can't take that long."

"It will if you have to eat every thirty minutes. Now go fix your sandwich and let's get this over with."

"You're a real bitch, you know," Phoebe shouted.

"Name-calling isn't going to change anything."

"Yeah. Well, maybe not. But this is still all your fault and you really are a bitch." She gave Fran a questioning look.

"What?"

"Do we have anything in the frig to make a sandwich? I think we finished the ham."

"There's some roast beef left from yesterday. Cut a few slices of that for your stupid sandwich."

"Oh, right. I forgot about that," Phoebe said. "Do you want me to make you one?"

"No, I don't want one."

"You sure?"

"I'm sure," Fran replied.

"Last chance," Phoebe called out as she walked towards the kitchen.

"Do you irritate me on purpose?" Fran called after her sister.

Phoebe smiled.

"Do you feel better now that you've had something to eat?"

"I guess. I think I'd like a drink," Phoebe told her.

"Then, have a drink, and let's get moving."

"I mean a real drink. Like whiskey or gin or something. It might help."

"Really? I don't know ..."

"I'm having one. You should, too. What do you want? I'm having a shot of whiskey."

"No way. It will knock you out and I'll have to do everything by myself," Fran told her.

"Just one isn't going to hurt anything. And, it might just relax you a little. You're so fricking uptight."

"I am not uptight"

"Do you want a drink or not?"

"I guess I could have one." Fran thought for a moment. "Okay, go get the whiskey. But, just one shot. Deal?"

"Deal."

"I'll get the garbage bags while you pour."

"Sounds like a plan," Phoebe said, grinning.

"These are lawn bags," Phoebe declared an hour later.

"They're a lot bigger. We should be able to get his arms in one bag and his legs in another."

"What about his head?" Phoebe asked.

"You mean his big fat ugly head?" She shivered as she looked at the man. "God, he's so ugly he makes me want to puke." She sat down on the toilet seat and thought. "I think a bag for his head and one for his torso. Yep, four should take care of it," Fran declared.

"Are you gonna cut off his wiener?" Phoebe asked giggling.

"Absolutely," Fran replied, laughing loudly.

"You could put that in a sandwich bag."

"A sandwich bag is too big. Do you have any of those little jewelry bags?" she asked, laughing hysterically now.

"I have a better idea," Phoebe said. "I think we should give it to the neighbor's dog."

"For a chew toy," Fran added, giggling for a moment. "Nooo, we can't do that. I like that dog," she said seriously. "He might choke on it." She reached for the bottle of whiskey. "Want another?"

"Another what?" Phoebe asked, looking confused

CHAPTER TWO

Tuesday, November 1st

"Wake up," Fran yelled, as she hit Phoebe on her shoulder.

Phoebe opened her right eye and gazed up at Fran. "Stop it. That hurts."

"Good. I need some help here, lady. I can't do this by myself. I told you that having a drink wasn't a good idea. You just couldn't stop at one, could you?"

"Thanks to you." Phoebe closed her left eye and burped. "I think I'm gonna be sick," she mumbled.

Fran stared down at her, realized she was serious, and opened the lid of the toilet. "Then puke, but do it in the toilet. And, for God's sake don't get any on the floor."

"Thank you," Phoebe said softly. "You always take such. . ."

Fran shook her head as Phoebe started to snore. "You have got to be kidding me," she muttered. She took a deep breath, grabbed Phoebe's feet, and pulled her out of the bathroom into the hallway. "Well, here goes nothing." She resisted the temptation to give Phoebe a kick in her ass and reached for the saw instead. "Ah, crap."

Phoebe looked over at Fran. "Whattaya doing?"

"I need to get some plastic to put under him."

"Do you want me to go to the store and get some?" Phoebe asked.

"Sure, why don't you take my car?"

Phoebe started to push herself up into a standing position. "What time should I be back?" she asked giving Fran a crooked smile.

Fran gave her a look, shaking her head in disgust. "Get your ass in your room and take a nap. I'm going to run to the hardware store and get some plastic."

"Sure, I can do that," Phoebe said, stumbling down the hallway.

"And, Pheebs..."

"What?" Phoebe asked, looking back at Fran.

"Do not – I repeat – do not answer the door or the phone. Under any circumstances. Understand?"

"What if it's mom?"

"Go lie down."

"Well? Should I let her in?"

"Mom is dead, Phoebe. Remember?"

"Oh, yeah. Right."

"Wait a minute." Fran reached for the wastebasket and handed it to Phoebe. "Take this in case you get sick."

As Fran started to back out of the driveway, she felt the car hit a bump. She hit the brakes and closed her eyes. *"Please, dear God, don't let that be a kid."* She opened her car door and looked toward the back of the car. She let out a sigh of relief, pulled the car forward a few feet, and jumped out.

She picked up a broom and tossed it onto the grass. *Damn trick-and-treaters,* she thought. *Looks like some kid lost part of her costume.*

She breathed in the cool night air, wondering what the hell she was doing. She had imbibed as many shots of whiskey as Phoebe and she sure as hell shouldn't be driving a car.

She got back into the driver's seat and pulled the car back into the garage. The plastic could wait until morning, she decided.

The following morning, at six o'clock sharp, Fran walked through the sliding glass doors and entered The Home Depot. She stood for a moment and looked around, trying to get her bearings. "Excuse me, where do you keep your plastic wrap?" she asked a floor assistant as he walked toward her.

"What kind of plastic wrap? For the kitchen or...?"

"Big and clear. The kind you use to cover stuff when you paint," Fran interrupted.

"It sounds like you want plastic sheeting. You'll find that in aisle 7," the man told her.

"Where's that?"

"Aisle 7 is to your right."

"Thanks," Fran said, as she walked away to look for aisle 7.

"Cash or charge?" the cashier asked.

"Cash," Fran said, handing her two twenty-dollar bills. No way she was going to leave a paper trail.

The cashier handed Fran her change. "Thank you."

"Damn stuff is expensive," Fran muttered, as she picked up her parcel and walked toward the door.

Fran walked into the house and threw the shopping bag on the couch. "You up?" she yelled.

"Don't make so much noise," Phoebe said, as she walked into the room carrying a cup of coffee.

"Headache?"

"What do you think?"

"Good. Now, put the cup down, and let's get busy."

"Can I finish my coffee first," Phoebe whined.

"No. Get upstairs and strip down to your panties and bra."

Phoebe gave her a questioning look. "Why?"

"The fewer clothes we have on, the less evidence we have to get rid of." She sighed. "Just do it, will you, Pheebs? We've got a lot of work to do today and I'd like to get started."

"All right. God, I hope you're not going to be like this all day."

"You can count on it. We'd be halfway through this mess if you hadn't got drunk and passed out last night."

"And, I wouldn't have passed out if you hadn't kept pouring more shots."

"All right. So, we're both to blame. Let's just forget it and get on with it."

"I'm not touching him," Phoebe stated.

"You most certainly are," Fran told her. "I'm not doing this alone."

"I want gloves. Do we have any?"

Fran thought for a moment. "I don't think so but you can check the utility room."

Phoebe turned and ran out of the room and down the stairs.

"Hurry up," Fran yelled. "She is going to drive me crazy," she mumbled to herself. She stared at the man on

10

the bathroom floor, wishing her mom was still alive. She would know what to do.

"We don't have any," Phoebe called up to Fran. "I'm going to run to the drug store and pick up a box of vinyl gloves."

"For crying out loud, Pheebs, do you really need them?"

"If you want help, I want gloves."

"Okay, but make it fast. If we keep putting this off the whole house is going to start to smell."

"All right! I'll be right back."

I think a cup of coffee would taste good right about now, Fran thought, as she heard Phoebe slam the door that led to the garage.

Fran felt sick to her stomach. She shouldn't have had the coffee before deciding to undress the man. Just touching his cold pale skin had given her the shivers. *If I feel this way by just touching the fat pig, how am I ever going to be able to slice and dice him? And, where the hell is Phoebe? She's been gone over forty-five minutes.*

"I'm back," Phoebe yelled, as she slammed the door shut.

"Where the hell have you been? The drug store is only five minutes away. What the hell took you so long?"

"Well, I see you're still in a good mood."

"Don't be a smart ass. Where were you?"

"I stopped at the bakery and picked up some fresh donuts. I got you your favorite."

"You what?" Fran asked, not believing what her sister had just told her.

"Jelly," Phoebe said. "Just the kind you like."

"Pheebs, let me tell you something. It's obvious that you don't understand that we have a situation here. There is a dead man in our bathroom. We have to get rid of the body before someone comes looking for him. Besides that, he is going to start to rot and stink to high heaven. You need to get your head out of your ass and start to concentrate on the job at hand. Got it?"

"Of course, I got it. What? Do you think I'm stupid or something?" Phoebe held out the bag from the donut shop. "You want one?"

Fran looked at her, glanced down at the bag, and yanked it out of Phoebe's hand. She reached inside and pulled out a jelly donut. "Just one."

"Do you want some coffee with that?" Phoebe asked, smiling.

CHAPTER THREE

"So, what's the plan?" Phoebe asked as she stood gazing down at the man on the bathroom floor.

"We need to push him toward the wall, lay the plastic sheet out, and roll him onto it. Once he's on the plastic, you can hold his arm while I saw it off."

"Do we have any masks? I think we should be wearing masks while we saw so we don't breathe in any of his bone dust."

"I'm getting..." Fran stopped talking and shook her head agreeing with Phoebe. "You're right. We should wear masks."

"I'll go get them." Phoebe turned and started toward the stairs.

"Wait. Where are you going?" Fran asked.

"To the store to get some masks."

"Oh, no, you aren't. You're not leaving this house again. I'll go get them while you push fatso closer to the wall. I'll be back in five."

"You aren't going to leave me alone with him, are you?"

"What's he gonna do, Pheebs? Jump up and bite you? Just try to push him across the room. Maybe rolling him will work. Why don't you give that a try?"

13

Phoebe stared at her, tears starting to fill her eyes. "Why can't I go with you?"

"Because one of us needs to stay here." Fran ran down the stairs and grabbed her car keys. "Don't answer the door or the phone. Got it?"

Phoebe shook her head up and down.

"Did you hear me?"

"I heard you," Phoebe yelled.

"I'll be right back. Now get to work."

Phoebe put her foot out and touched the man with her toe. She pulled back her foot and made a face. "Gross," she muttered. She thought for a moment, then went downstairs. She grabbed a broom from the kitchen and went back up to the bathroom. Standing on the right side of the man, she took the broom, shoved it into his side, and pushed. He didn't move.

Phoebe wedged the broom handle under the man, hoping that if she pushed up on the handle, he would roll toward the wall. No matter how hard she pushed, the man did not move.

She glanced over at the box of gloves and decided she better glove up before she touched him. She slipped on a pair of vinyl gloves, walked over to the man, and bent down facing his right side. Using both hands, she pushed with all her strength, trying to roll him onto his stomach. He moved a few inches to his left and then rolled back to where he had been.

"Shit!" she exclaimed. She sat there trying to catch her breath. "I got it!" she suddenly exclaimed. She sat down on the floor, her back against the tub, and, using both feet, pushed as hard as she could. The man moved toward the wall about six inches. "Good. That was good."

14

She pushed again and he slid another six inches. She stopped and listened, hearing a noise downstairs. "Is that you, Fran?" she called out.

"It's me. I'll be right up."

"I moved him," Phoebe yelled.

"That's it? It took you this long to move him a couple of inches?"

Phoebe pulled herself up and looked Fran in the eyes. "All right, miss smarty pants, let's see you do any better."

Fran gloved up, bent down, and tried to push the man closer to the wall.

"Well? What are you waiting for?" Phoebe asked, a smirky grin on her face. "Isn't so easy, is it?"

Fran glanced over at her. "Okay, you win. Now get down here and help me push."

Phoebe joined her sister on the floor and the two women managed to push the dead man almost the entire distance to the opposite wall.

"That's enough," Fran said, puffing from exhaustion. "God, he must weigh a ton."

"Now what?"

"Spread out the plastic and we'll roll him back onto it."

"I gotta rest a minute," Phoebe told her.

"I need a drink of water. What about you?" Fran asked.

"Sounds good. With a little ice if you don't mind."

"Ready?" Phoebe asked her sister.

"Ready as I'll ever be."

"Okay. Push!"

15

The man rolled onto his stomach, landing in the middle of the plastic sheeting, expelling air from his rectum that mimicked someone blowing a raspberry.

Fran fell backward against the wall. "What the hell was that?"

Phoebe stared at the man's ass for a moment and then started to laugh. "He farted. I didn't know dead people farted."

Suddenly, Fran jumped up and ran toward the door. "Oh, my God! Oh, that's horrible." She looked at Phoebe. "Get out while you can. That smell is going to kill you." She fell to the floor outside the bathroom, laughing. "Hurry, Pheebs."

Phoebe joined her on the floor, laughing so hard that tears filled her eyes. "That has to be the most repugnant, foul, nauseating smell I have ever smelled," she declared. "Let's get out of here before we're overcome by the odor and die."

"Hit the fan switch and let's go," Fran said.

Twenty minutes later Phoebe looked over at Fran and smiled. "We did it."

"We sure did."

"Does it make any difference that he's on his stomach? Can we still separate him that way?"

"It will probably be easier not having to look at his face."

"What should we cut off first?" Phoebe asked her.

"Left leg."

"I thought we were gonna do an arm first."

"I changed my mind. I'm not sure if I should do it in two pieces or one."

"Do you want me to google it?"

Fran held back a laugh. "What are you going to type in the search box, if I may be so bold as to ask?"

"I think you should start above the knee. Or, maybe below it."

"Okay," Fran replied. "Then what?"

"Then, the other leg. Then, the arms, the head, the thighs. Oh, I know," she added excitedly.

"What do you know?" Fran asked her.

"We should cut off the hands and feet and bag them separately. Maybe we could burn them. That way they can't get the fingerprints and footprints if they find the bags."

"Footprints. Who takes footprints?"

"The hospital does after a baby is born."

Fran shook her head in agreement. "Right. Okay, let's get started. I'll do a foot first, just to see how it goes."

"Do you want me to hold the foot while you saw it off?"

Fran thought about it for a moment. "I think it would be better if you held the leg still. Can you do that?"

"Sure. Do you want a mask?" Phoebe asked, holding one out for Fran to take.

"Thanks." She put on the mask and reached for the saw that was lying next to her. "Well, here goes nothing."

Phoebe watched as Fran placed the saw on the man's ankle and started pushing it back and forth, cutting through the skin. "It's working," she cried out.

"Of course, it working. I haven't hit bone yet. That's when it's gonna get hard." Suddenly, the saw made a screeching noise as Fran cut into the ankle bone.

"You did it," Phoebe exclaimed.

"Just hold the leg still, please, and don't get excited." Fran continued to push the saw back and forth, hoping that the ankle would come detached from the leg. After almost five minutes, she stopped and sat back on her haunches.

"What's the matter?"

"I don't think this saw is gonna cut it. Do me a favor and go look up what type of saw is best for cutting bone, will you?"

Phoebe gave her a puzzling look. "Well, wouldn't that be a bone saw?"

"I imagine it would," Fran replied slowly and very patiently, trying not to lose her cool. "But we can't buy a bone saw in just any store in town, can we? So, find out what is the next best thing, please."

Fran walked down an aisle in Menards looking at the different types of saws. She was looking for a hacksaw, which the internet said was the closest thing to a bone saw. She finally decided on the one she thought she should buy and put it, plus several new saw blades, in her cart. It was the most expensive one in the store, so she figured it should be the best.

She checked out and walked to her car. *This is becoming a nightmare*, she thought. *This damn well better work.*

"Fran, come here. Hurry," Phoebe yelled out as soon as Fran walked into the living room.

"Let me take my coat off first, will you?" Fran yelled back. She threw her coat on a chair and walked upstairs to the bathroom. "What?"

"Look," Phoebe said proudly, pointing to a footless leg. "I did it."

"How the hell did you do it?"

18

"I found an ax in the garage," Phoebe said, pointing to the ax on the floor. "Two good swings and it was off."

"That's good, Pheebs, but I'm not sure that's going to work for the rest of the body."

"Why not? You saw through the skin and I'll swing the ax. We can be done with this in no time."

"I don't know, Pheebs."

"What's not to know?"

"It's gonna be super messy."

"We can at least give it a try. You said you wanted to get this done, so let's get moving."

"Let me try the new saw first. This one might work better."

"All right. But if it doesn't work, I'm going at it with the ax."

Fran unwrapped the saw from its packaging, checked the blade, and got down on her knees.

"Wait," Phoebe said.

"What?"

"You have to take your clothes off first. Remember?"

CHAPTER FOUR

"This is taking way too long," Fran stated, as she sat back on her heels.

"I agree. We've still got a lot to..." Phoebe glanced over at Fran. "Was that the doorbell?"

"I think so."

"What should we do?"

"Nothing. Just stay quiet and they'll go away."

"Did you put your car in the garage?" Phoebe asked.

"Yeah. Nobody knows we're here."

The two women waited a few moments until they were pretty sure that the person at the door had left. "I'm going to go check and make sure the front door is locked," Fran told Phoebe. "We don't need anyone trying to get in."

"Who do you think it was?"

"Not a clue."

"Do you think someone is looking for him?" Phoebe asked.

"Probably." Fran stood up and stretched. "God, this is hard on my back." She jumped as something touched her leg. "God, Sammy, you scared me," she declared, laughing nervously, as she reached down and picked up a big gray fluffy cat. "Have you fed him today?" she asked Phoebe.

"I fed him this morning."

Fran petted the cat for a few seconds before putting him back on the floor. "He just needed a little love," she declared.

"Don't we all?" Phoebe asked.

"Please, stop," Fran said. "It isn't working. You're just wearing yourself out."

Phoebe dropped the ax to the floor and took a deep breath. "You're right," she said, as she let her breath out. "His damn bones are too hard."

"Or, perhaps, you're too weak."

"If you recall, I did manage to get the one foot off." She stared at Swinger's torso. "I guess it could have been a fluke. What are we going to do now?" Phoebe asked.

"I've got one more idea but it means another trip to the hardware store. I'm getting a chain saw. If they can cut trees down, they sure as hell should cut through this fat ass's bones."

"Do you want me to google it and check it out?" Phoebe asked.

"See if they make electric ones. I don't want to have to buy a gas can and then drive to the gas station and get gas. Too many trips and too many trails to follow."

"I'll be right back," Phoebe told her.

Fran took off her gloves and went to the sink. She washed her hands and arms and checked her face in the mirror to be sure there weren't any skin or bone particles sticking to her. She went out to the hallway, picked up her clothes, and dressed. "Did you find anything?" she called out to Phoebe.

"They make electric ones. We'll need a heavy-duty extension cord, though. Do we have any here?"

"We have a couple in the garage."

Phoebe walked out of the room they used as a den and looked at her sister. "Take a moment and put on some lipstick and maybe comb your hair. You look kind of bedraggled."

"I know. Thanks, Pheebs."

"I'm going to clean up the kitchen while you're gone. Maybe make a sandwich. Do you want me to fix you something?"

"Actually, I am hungry. Do we have any eggs?"

"I think so."

"I'm in the mood for an egg salad sandwich. Do you want to make a couple?"

"Sure thing. Anything else?"

"Maybe while you're messing around in there, you could check and see what we need at the grocery store. It's been a while since we shopped and we're running low on food."

"That took a long time," Phoebe commented when Fran walked into the kitchen.

"I went to Lowes. Their store is farther than Menards and Home Depot."

She looked around the kitchen. "The kitchen looks nice. Good job, Pheebs."

"Thanks. Lunch is ready."

"Now don't freak out," Fran said as she sat down at the table and picked up her sandwich, "but I got stopped by the police as I was pulling out of the driveway."

Phoebe stared at her, her face turning pale. She grabbed the edge of the counter to steady herself. "Did you say the police?" she asked, her voice trembling.

"I did."

"Oh, shit! Oh, God. Why? What did you do? What did you say?" She took a deep breath.

"Steady there. You're gonna give yourself a heart attack. Everything is okay."

"Oh, my God," Phoebe exclaimed, feeling her chest with her hand. "My heart is beating so fast." She took another deep breath and let it out. "What did they want?"

"The police were canvassing the neighborhood. They are concerned because Pastor Swinger's car has been parked down the street for a couple of days. No one has seen him since the afternoon of Halloween and the church secretary is concerned."

Phoebe waited for more information. "What did you tell him?" she finally asked.

"I know nothing," Fran told her grinning. "Just like Sergeant Schultz."

"Who?" Phoebe asked.

"You know, Pheebs. The guy from Hogan's Heroes."

Phoebe smiled. "Of course. I forgot about that show. Good answer, Fran."

"Anyway, the cop seemed satisfied. Hopefully, we won't be hearing from him again."

"Did you get the saw?" Phoebe asked, changing the subject.

"I did. I also picked up some beer for later and some cold cuts. I think we have enough bread for a day or two."

"You're a doll. I could go for a beer right now."

"Sorry, it's for later. We aren't going to have a repeat of the other night."

"Hold the bag open," Phoebe told Fran, as she picked up what was left of a hand.

Fran spread the opening of the black garbage bag as wide as she could and watched Phoebe drop the man's right hand into the bag. "God, he's really starting to stink," Fran declared.

"What's in what bag? I've lost track," Phoebe asked.

"His feet and hands are in the bag I'm holding. His fingers are in that bag over there," Fran replied.

Phoebe glanced toward the bag Fran was looking at and froze. "Don't move," she whispered.

Fran looked puzzled. "Why?"

"That bag is moving. Oh, my God, Fran. His fingers are moving. We need to get out of here."

Fran reached over and pulled the bag closer. She opened it and reached inside. "Oh, Sammy, how did you get in there?" She lifted the cat out of the bag and handed him to Phoebe. "It's just Sammy. Here, take him."

"No. Oh, no!" Phoebe shouted. "Make him drop that."

Fran turned the cat around and looked at his face. "Ah, shit! Drop it, Sammy. Let go." She grabbed the finger sticking out of his mouth and pulled. Sammy, having other ideas, wiggled and squirmed his way out of her hands, hit the floor, and took off running. He passed Phoebe, ran into the hallway, and down the stairs, holding the severed finger tight between his teeth.

"We've got to get that finger," Fran said, sighing.

"I know. It will make him sick if he eats it."

The two women stood up and headed down the stairs.

"What time is it?" Phoebe asked.

"Time for a frickin' nap. I'm beat," Fran replied.

"I want a beer."

"I'll get 'em." Fran got off the couch and went to the kitchen. A moment later Phoebe heard her yell out.

"What's the matter?"

"The damn cat threw up all over the floor."

"Well, clean it up. He's your cat."

Fran walked back into the living room and handed her sister a beer. "I'll do it later."

"Thanks," Phoebe said.

"I'm tired, Pheebs. This is all starting to get to me. I don't want to do this anymore."

"I know. I'm tired, too. But we haven't got a choice, do we?"

Fran took a long sip of beer. "That hit the spot."

"How about we order some take-out? We need to eat something besides sandwiches. Besides, people know we're here. We have to act normal and not hide inside the house."

Fran sat back and rested her head against the back of the couch. "You're right. You pick something. I'm gonna take a five-minute nap."

Phoebe glanced over at her sister and smiled. Fran was out like a light. *Man, I wish I could fall asleep like that*, she thought. She watched as Sammy jumped up on the couch and snuggled close to Fran, purring so loud you could hear him across the room. *I'll give her fifteen minutes*, Phoebe thought. *Then we've got to get back to work.* She laid her head back against the cushion and started to close her eyes. Suddenly, she jerked upright and stared at Sammy. He was licking the severed finger, holding it upright between his paws. "Psst, Fran. Fran," Phoebe whispered. "Wake up."

Fran opened her eyes and looked at Phoebe. "Sorry. I guess I nodded off for a moment."

"Very slowly reach down and grab the finger away from Sammy," Phoebe said softly.

"Do what?"

"Sammy's next to you and he's got the finger."

Fran looked at Sammy. "Brazen little shit, isn't he?"

"Just take the finger."

Fran reached for the finger. Sammy continued to gaze at Phoebe while licking his prize, totally ignoring Fran. Just as Fran tried to grab the finger away from him, Sammy hissed, jumped off the couch, and ran under the table.

"Does he still have it?" Fran asked.

"I swear he's laughing at us," Phoebe told her.

"I gather that's a yes."

CHAPTER FIVE

"Maybe he ate some of it and it made him sick," Phoebe said. "You need to check it out."

"Why me?"

"It's your cat, Fran."

The two women walked into the kitchen and stared at the floor. "That's a lot of puke," Phoebe said, stating the obvious.

"It's pretty runny," Fran commented, bending down to get a closer look at the vomit. "I don't think there's any part of a finger here. I don't see any bone mixed in." She straightened up and reached for the paper towels on the counter. "I'm gonna clean this up." She grinned. "Do you want to help?"

"Not funny. I'm out of here. God, that stinks. How can you stand it?"

Fran shrugged. "I don't know. Nothing about Sammy bothers me. He's like my baby. You get used to it and you do what you need to do." She tore a bunch of towels off of the roll, bent down, and started to wipe up the vomit.

Phoebe took one look at what her sister was doing and gagged. "I'm out of here," she said. "I'll look for the finger in the other room."

"Did you find it?" Fran asked as she walked into the living room.

"Nope. I don't think it's in this room. God only knows where he might have hidden it. He has a million hiding places."

"He is a busy little boy, aren't you, Sammy?" Fran said, looking at the cat sleeping on the couch. "I guess we should get back to work. Ready?"

"As ready as I'll ever be."

"He doesn't look as stiff as he did before," Phoebe commented.

"The rigor mortis is probably wearing off. He'll be soft again in a few hours."

"Will it be easier to cut him up when he's soft?"

"I don't think it makes any difference. Bone is bone, stiff body or not."

"Fran..." Phoebe hesitated.

"What?"

"Never mind."

"Come on. Out with it? What were you going to ask me?"

"How come his pecker didn't get stiff like the rest of him? It stayed the same size." She giggled. "Which is what I'd call a small."

"It's something to do with muscles stiffening up. I guess the peter doesn't have muscles."

"How do you know that?"

"I read a lot, okay?"

"He sure has a little pecker considering what a big man he is," Phoebe declared.

"How about we get to work and you quit fixating on his penis?"

"I guess. Just remember, though, that it's his penis that got him into all this trouble."

"I know. But we need to forget about that now, Pheebs."

"Right." Phoebe took a deep breath and let it out. "What next?"

"How about we take off the arms?" Fran plugged the extension cord into the wall socket and powered up the saw. "Yes," she yelled. "Now we're cooking."

"Pastor Swinger, how are you?" Phoebe asked as she opened the front door.

"I'm fine, my dear. Did I catch you at a bad time?"

"Not at all. Well, maybe a little. I was just about to take some cookies out of the oven."

"Well, don't let me stop you. I wanted to check and see how you and your sister are doing. I've been concerned about you and Fran since your mother died. Do you need anything?"

"We're getting along okay. It's hard not having her around, though."

"I would imagine. She was such a wonderful woman. Well, I'll just sit down and wait for you to finish up in the kitchen," he said, as he pushed his way by her and headed toward the couch.

Phoebe stood by the open door for a moment, wondering what was up. She closed the door and walked toward the kitchen. "I'll be right back," she told him. "I need to get those cookies out of the oven before they burn."

"What type of cookies are you making, my dear?"

"Good old-fashioned oatmeal," Phoebe replied. "If you'll just excuse me..."

"Of course. Of course. Go – do your cookie thing," Swinger told her smiling.

Phoebe went into the kitchen, put on her oven mitts, and opened the oven door. As she reached down to pull the cookie sheet out of the oven, she felt a hand grab her ass. "What the hell do you think you're doing?" she yelled, holding onto the cookie sheet as she turned toward the man.

Swinger started to back up but Phoebe had already raised the hot cookie sheet. She brought it down hard, hitting him on top of his head. He cried out as she hit him again. On her third attempt to clobber him, he punched her in the stomach, knocking the wind out of her. She doubled over and fell to the floor.

Swinger stared down at her, saliva drooling out of his mouth and down his chin. "You little bitch. That hurt," he yelled. "You've sinned against a man of God and now you must do your penance." He unzipped his fly, dropped to his knees, and grabbed her by her hair, forcing her head toward his crotch.

Fran reached over and shook Phoebe's shoulder. "Pheebs? Are you okay?"

Phoebe glanced over at her, looking surprised. "What?"

"You went away for a minute there. What the hell were you thinking about?"

Phoebe shook her head. "Nothing. I guess I just zoned out for a moment."

"You were thinking about what Swinger did, weren't you?"

"I guess."

30

"Get it out of your mind, Pheebs, or you'll drive yourself nuts."

"That's a lot easier to say than do, you know. Especially when the fat pig is right in front of me."

"Try to block it out for now, if you can. Okay?" Fran asked.

Phoebe smiled. "Okay. Sorry."

Fran looked at Swinger, calculating her next move. "I think it will be easier to cut the arms off if we turn him over. It shouldn't be hard to move him now without his legs."

"I guess," Phoebe agreed. "Let's do it."

The two women rolled the man over onto his back. "That looks good," Fran declared. "Hold his arm out as far as you can."

Phoebe took Swinger's arm and held it tight while Fran stood over him and cut his arm off.

Phoebe looked at her, shocked. "My God, that was so easy. Do the other one now."

Fran grinned. "Hold it for me."

"You're a natural with that saw, you know. I never knew you had it in you, Fran."

As soon as the second arm joined the first arm in the black lawn bag, Phoebe stood up. "I'll be right back," she told her sister.

"Where are you going?"

"Just wait. I'll be right back."

Fran watched her sister run out of the bathroom and sighed. "God only knows what she's up to now," she murmured.

"What the hell are you doing with that?" Fran asked as Phoebe walked back into the bathroom.

31

"I'm cutting it off."

"Cutting what off? You've got the pruning shears. What do..." Fran stopped talking as the realization of what Phoebe was going to do hit home. "You're not."

"Like hell, I'm not. Watch this." Phoebe double-gloved her left hand, reached over, and pulled Swinger's penis to its full length. "Pretty small, isn't it?" she said grinning. Holding the shears in her right hand, she wrapped the cutting blades around his penis and squeezed as hard as she could.

"I can't watch this," Fran said, looking away.

"Done and done," Phoebe cried out, watching the detached member fall between Swinger's thighs.

"You're sick, you know that?" Fran inquired.

"Really. Who's the sick one? Me or him? I didn't try to rape him, did I? So, I guess that leaves him.

Fran opened the lawn bag. "Toss it in here."

Phoebe looked at Swinger's member. "I don't want to touch it again. You do it."

Fran reached between the man's legs and gingerly picked up his penis. "I don't understand how men can walk around with these things dangling between their legs. I'm so glad I was born a girl."

"At what age do you think their brains migrate down there?" Phoebe asked, grinning.

Fran laughed. "Well, from my experience, they're born with them down there."

CHAPTER SIX

"We should get rid of those three bags before we do the rest."

"I don't know if we should leave the house. I think we should finish up and dump everything at the same time," Phoebe said. "He's going to stink worse every hour he's up there."

Fran took a bite of her pizza and chewed, thinking about what to do. "No, we have to get rid of them. We'll close the door and turn on the fan. If we are only gone a couple of hours, it shouldn't be that much worse than it is now."

"Where do you think we should dump the bags?"

"I think in three different places, no farther than an hour away. Maybe we dump one outside of Janesville. That's less than an hour if we take I90. We could head back on Hwy 14 and dump the other two in the woods on the way home."

"It's gonna be dark, you know."

"I know. That's what we want."

"What woods? Do you know where to go?"

"Pheebs, we've lived here all our lives. I know those roads like the back of my hand. No problem. I know exactly where to go."

"What about the rest of him? Where are we gonna put the rest of the bags?"

"We go north, Pheebs. We'll spread him around."

Phoebe grinned. "Well, there is enough of him to cover the whole state. Okay. Let's put the bags in the trunk."

"Good girl. We'll be back in two hours and we'll finish the job."

"In another two hours, I'm going to want a nap."

"Do you want any more pizza?"

"Nope. I'm full."

Fran smiled at her sister. "You've been really good about all this, Pheebs. I'm so sorry what happened to you."

Phoebe smiled back and shrugged. "Me, too. But what's done is done. Plus, it could have been worse, you know."

"Leave your phone here. I'm going to disable the GPS on mine so we can't be tracked."

"What about your car?"

"That quit working six months ago."

"How come you never said anything?" Phoebe asked.

"I don't know. I guess it wasn't important."

"Do you think we could stop and get a cup of coffee?" Phoebe asked yawning.

"I guess. Evansville is right up the road from here. There should be a McDonald's or something there."

"How do you know about all those back roads, Fran? I don't think I could find them during the day and you drove right to them."

Fran smiled. "Do you remember when I dated that boy from Union?"

"Yeah. His name was Matthew... No, it was Mitch. Right?"

"Close. It was Michael. Michael John Smith."

"That's right."

"We did a lot of parking back in those days. Plus, it's a well-known secret with the high schoolers that there are a few small lakes back in that area. We used to go swimming there during the summer."

"Skinny dipping?"

Fran laughed. "Maybe a couple of times. We had a lot of good parties back in those days."

"It wasn't that long ago, Fran."

"I guess. But it seems like ages ago."

Phoebe laid her head against the back of the seat and closed her eyes. After a few moments, Fran glanced over at her and frowned. "Oh, no, you don't. You don't get to sleep until I do."

"I wasn't sleeping. I was thinking."

"Yeah, right."

"When does Gary get home?"

"Next week sometime. I can't wait to see him. It seems like he's been gone forever."

"Well, six months is a long time. You aren't going to tell him anything, are you?"

"Are you crazy? Of course not. No one must ever know what happened, Pheebs. You have to promise me."

"Of course, I promise. I would never say anything."

"Here's Evansville. Watch for a place to get some coffee." Fran looked into her rearview mirror. "Oh, shit," she exclaimed. "I've got a cop behind me."

"So?" Phoebe asked. "You haven't done anything wrong."

"He just turned his lights on. I've got to pull over. Let me do the talking."

Fran pulled her car over to the side of the road and opened her window. "God, I hate this," she whispered to her sister.

She looked over as a police officer approached her window. "Evening, Officer."

"Ma'am. Do you know how fast you were going?"

"I believe I was doing thirty-five. Isn't that the speed limit? I thought I saw a sign."

"Yes, you were," replied smiling. "And, good for you."

"If I wasn't speeding, why did you pull me over?" Fran asked, confused by the officer's answer.

"Gotcha!" he said, grinning. "Actually, you have a light out, ma'am. Your left tail light."

Fran let out her breath. "I didn't know. I'll get it fixed as soon as possible."

"I should give you a warning ticket, but if you promise to get it fixed first thing in the morning, I'll give you a pass."

"I promise. Absolutely. I will get it fixed."

"Where are you two ladies going, anyway?"

"Madison. We live there."

"Well, good for you. You drive safe now, you hear."

"Yes, Sir. Absolutely. Thank you."

Fran waited until the cop drove off before she started her car. "That went well," she said.

Phoebe didn't answer her.

"Pheebs?"

Phoebe opened the car door, jumped out, and threw up on the side of the road.

"Atta girl," Fran yelled. "You managed to hold it until the cop left."

"Shut up, Fran."

"Bathroom door shut, fan going, and it's not doing a thing."

Fran walked into the living room and made a face. "You're right. We have to get the rest of him out of here tonight."

Phoebe sighed and plumped down on the couch. "I'm so tired," she whined.

"Quit complaining, will you?"

"Sammy's still sleeping," Phoebe commented, as she looked at the cat lying next to her. She started to pet him and pulled her hand back. "Fran?"

"What now?"

"I don't think Sammy is sleeping. I think he's dead."

"No!" Fran cried out. "He can't be." She reached over and shook the cat. "Sammy, wake up." She looked at Phoebe, her eyes begging for help. "Do something," she yelled. "Help me."

"He's gone, Fran. There's nothing I can do."

Fran fell to her knees crying. "My baby is gone. Oh, Sammy, you poor thing. I left you all alone to die." She pulled her cat close to her and held it. "My poor, poor baby."

"Do you think he's been here since we left?" Phoebe asked.

"What... what do... do you mean, here?" Fran asked between her sobs."

"On the couch."

"How should I know." She looked at Phoebe, tears rolling down her cheeks. "What difference does it make?"

"The finger is gone. If he didn't move it, maybe he ate it. We need to know where that finger is, Fran."

Fran stared at her. "What are you saying, Pheebs?"

"I think you know. We have to find out for sure if Sammy ate that finger."

"No way in hell!"

"I'll do it," Phoebe told her. "You don't have to be there."

"You couldn't even look at Sammy's vomit without gagging and now you think you can cut his guts open? I highly doubt it."

"It has to be done. We have to find that finger."

"No," Fran cried out, pulling her dead cat closer to her chest. "You're not cutting him open."

"Take some time, Fran, and think about it. We can search the house again, but if we don't find it – well, I don't see any other choice. In the meantime, we have work to do upstairs."

Fran stared at her sister, shocked by what she had suggested.

"Come on. Let's get this shit over with and try to get back to some semblance of normality," Phoebe said. Fran continued to stare at her. "Now, Fran. Put the damn cat down and let's get moving."

Fran glared at her. "You never did like him, did you? You were never nice to him."

"I'm sorry. I shouldn't have said that. You know that cat dander makes my allergies go nuts. That's why I hardly ever touched him. He was a good cat and I'm sorry he's dead. Besides, he was old. He probably would have died soon anyway."

Fran rolled her eyes. "You give and then you take away."

"I'm sorry. That might have come out the wrong way. I really am sorry, Fran. But we need to finish the job upstairs."

"I have to bury Sammy first," Fran said, still crying.

"You can bury him later. Just let him rest on the couch for now. We'll give him a real nice funeral when we get back. I'll dig a hole in the back yard and you can wrap him in his favorite blanket and we'll say a prayer for him. How about that?"

Fran wiped her eyes with the back of her hand. "He should have Mousey with him. He loved Mousey."

"Anything you want. We'll bury all of his toys with him if you want. But, let's do it later. Okay?"

"Okay." Fran gently laid Sammy down on the couch and covered him with an afghan. She stroked his back and whispered, "I love you, Sammy. Sleep tight."

CHAPTER SEVEN

Wednesday, November 2nd

"Why aren't you using the chain saw?"

"I think this will work to take his head off. Plus, it's not as messy."

Phoebe looked around the bathroom. "We have a lot of cleaning up to do, Fran. The chainsaw worked well, but it made one hell of a mess."

"I know," Fran said, as she pushed and pulled the hack saw back and forth. "I wish his eyes were closed. He's starting to freak me out."

"Wait." Phoebe grabbed a towel and placed it over Swinger's face. "Is that better?"

"Much. Thanks."

Phoebe watched as her sister severed the man's head. She stared at it for a moment and, then, kicked it.

"What the hell, Pheebs! What do you think you're doing?"

Phoebe shrugged. "That felt good and I'd do it again if I thought the bastard would feel it."

"Open the bag, will you?" Fran grabbed the head by the ears and dropped it into the bag. "We should have covered his face to begin with. It's better without him staring at us."

"We're done. Thank God. Let's bag the rest of him and get him out of here."

Fran stood up and stretched. She looked at Swinger's torso. "Houston, I think we have a problem," she said.

"What now?" Phoebe inquired.

"I don't think the rest of him is going to fit in one bag. Plus, I doubt we could lift it if it did."

"What – are – you - saying?" Phoebe asked, drawing out her question.

Fran sighed. "We may have to cut him in half."

"No fucking way! It's one thing to cut off his arms and legs and stuff, but cutting through his guts? No fucking way."

"We may not have a choice, Pheebs. Besides, it will be good practice for you."

"What do you mean – good practice?"

"You were the one talking about cutting my poor little Sammy open to search for that finger. If you can't do this, you sure as hell aren't going to be able to do that."

"Let's see if he'll fit in the bag first."

"Let's see if we can lift him first," Fran responded. "I suggest we triple glove. He's starting to get a little slimy."

Phoebe sat down on the edge of the bathtub and started to cry. "I can't do this," she whimpered.

"No choice, sister. You grab one end and I'll grab the other."

Fran pulled her hair back from her face and spit into the toilet bowl. "Mouthwash," she mumbled.

Phoebe handed her the bottle and tried to keep from laughing.

41

"How do you feel?" she asked.

"How do you think?" Fran sat back on her heels and took a deep breath. "That was terrible. I never want to do anything like that again."

"It was kind of gross with those intestines falling all over the place."

"Shut the fuck up!" Fran yelled. "I don't want to talk about it. He's bagged and ready to go. That's all that matters."

"How much do you think he weighed?" Phoebe asked. "I mean when he was still one piece."

"How should I know? Three, three-fifty? Maybe more?"

"Let's get these bags in the trunk. We can spend the next few hours cleaning this place."

"And, ourselves," Fran added. "We're covered with pieces of guts and stuff." She shivered. "Thank God this nightmare is almost over."

Phoebe reached over and put the stopper in the drain. She turned on the hot water and watched as it began to fill the tub.

"What are you doing? You can't take a bath yet?"

"We're gonna need a lot of bleach and rags. It will be easier to use the tub than buckets. And that way we can let it all go down the drain."

"I don't know, Pheebs. There are some pretty good-sized chunks splattered around."

"We can put some cloth over the drain and filter the water. That way we can catch the larger pieces. We'll use another bag for the leftovers and the rags."

"Sounds okay, I guess," Fran agreed. "Well, let's get him downstairs and into the car."

Three hours later, the two women stood in the bathroom doorway and inspected the room. "I think it looks good," Fran said.

"Me, too. I don't think we missed anything."

"We'll need to get some more bleach."

"Why?"

"To put down the drain after we shower. We want to be sure no particles of anything are stuck to the inside of the drain."

"We need to throw our panties and bras away, too." Phoebe sighed. "Do you think we'll ever be the same, Fran?"

"I doubt it. I'm already having nightmares and we've barely slept for three days."

"After tonight it will be better. Tomorrow is a new day and we need to put this behind us," Phoebe declared.

Fran looked at her sister and smiled.

"What?" Phoebe asked.

"When did you get so smart?"

Phoebe grinned. "It was bound to happen sooner or later. I guess some of my brain cells have decided to wake up."

"It's all yours," Fran told Phoebe as she walked out of the bathroom. "I'm going to get dressed and run to the store for more bleach."

"Thanks. I think I'll take a bath. I need to soak in hot water and try to loosen up my muscles."

"Do we need anything else from the store?" Fran asked.

"A bunch of stuff but it can wait until we do the grocery shopping later. I think we're okay for now."

"Good. I'll see you later."

As Phoebe started to walk into the bathroom, she turned back toward Fran. "By the way, if you happen to see any cookie sheets, we could use a new one."

"I'm glad to see you've got your sense of humor back," she said smiling.

Phoebe filled the tub with water. She stepped out of her panties, took her bra off, and put them in a bag. She stepped into the tub, laid her head back, sighed deeply, and closed her eyes.

Phoebe bit down as hard as she could, hoping Swinger would let go of her hair. He screamed and pulled away. Phoebe let go, rolling to her side. She kicked out with her feet and landed a solid hit on the man's cheek.

"You bitch," he yelled. "You could have bitten it off."

"I wish I had, you pervert," Phoebe yelled back, moving farther away from him. As she started to stand up, he grabbed her ankle and pulled her back toward him.

"No, you don't," he said. "I'm not done with you yet."

"Let go of me," Phoebe screamed. "What's wrong with you?"

Swinger slapped her across the face. "Stop fighting me."

She tried to twist out of his grasp, thrashing back and forth. He pushed her over on her side, shoved her face down onto the floor, and threw a leg over her back. Grabbing her arms, he pinned her so she couldn't move. "That's better," he murmured, putting his face close to her ear.

Hard as she tried, she couldn't move. His weight was practically crushing her. She tried to fight him but it was no use. He let go of one of her arms, reached down, and slid his hand into her pants.

"Get off me, you pig," Phoebe yelled, tears filling her eyes as she started to cry. "I'm gonna fucking kill you,"

"Now is that any way for a nice Christian girl like you to talk? I may have to give you a spanking."

Phoebe tried to twist away from him, crying harder now.

Swinger laughed. "I like it when my girls have a little spirit. It makes it so much fun." He stuck his tongue in her ear and licked it.

Phoebe shuddered. "Get the hell off me."

"You liked that, didn't you? I can tell you want more."

"I think I'm going to be sick," Phoebe said. "You're smothering me. I'm gonna throw up." She made a gagging noise and coughed.

Swinger pulled his hand out of her pants and rolled off of her. "Don't you throw up on me, you little bitch."

"Now!" Phoebe screamed. "Do it now!"

CHAPTER EIGHT

Wednesday, November 3rd

"Gary called," Fran told her sister.

"That's nice. Did he call for any special reason?"

"Just to say hi. Well, he did mention that he had a surprise for me."

"I just bet he does," Phoebe replied, grinning.

"Get your mind out of the gutter," Fran said. "Are you hungry?"

"I'm always hungry. Why?"

"We've got a few hours to kill before we – you know. I thought we might go to Chili's and get a bite to eat. I'm craving their chicken fingers."

"We could do that $20.00 thing."

"You mean the two for $25.00? It went up in price."

"You're kidding," Phoebe said. She shrugged. "Well, I guess it was bound to happen sooner or later. It stayed around $20.00 for quite a while."

"So, Chili's it is?"

"Sounds okay. I'll just be a minute. I want to take a look in the mirror first and see if I need a repair job before we leave."

"I think we should take your car," Fran said.

"Really, Fran? That's a no-brainer. If we take your car, we'll have every vulture in a five-mile radius following us."

"Make a mental note to be sure that we bring the air spray and masks with us. And, gloves," she added.

"I can't believe this nightmare will be over tonight. How far north are we going?"

"I think we should head toward Mauston and Necedah. There are a lot of side roads and woods in that area."

"I remember. If Castle River Lake isn't frozen over yet, we. . ."

"It won't be," Fran interrupted. "It's too early. Anyway, I don't think it's deep enough to hide a body."

"It's deep enough," Phoebe disagreed. "Do you know how many people have drowned in that lake?"

"A lot. But only because they didn't know how to swim or, if they did, they were too drunk to remember how. A person can drown in a foot of water, you know."

"I guess," Phoebe agreed. "If we toss the bags in the woods, the animals may have a meal or two. That would be good."

"Okay, then. Let's go eat," Fran said. "I'm starving."

Phoebe stopped the car in the driveway and waited for the garage door to open. She pulled into the garage and made a face. "My God, Fran. Maybe we should take some back roads out of town. The smell is horrible."

"I'm going to spray my car with that corpse odor eliminator before we leave," Fran told her. "We can run in and change clothes while it takes some of the smell away."

"Does that stuff work? "

"It's supposed to. I think it's called Smelleze. They use it in funeral homes and hospitals."

47

"Well, we'll find out, won't we?" Phoebe commented. "We can put a bowl of vinegar and baking soda in the trunk after we get back and let that sit for a while. I heard that helps to permanently get rid of the smell."

"We should do that in the bathroom before we leave, too," Fran said.

"Good idea."

"You might want to throw a change of clothes in a bag."

"Why?" Phoebe inquired.

"It was gonna be a surprise, but I guess I should tell you. We need to take a change of clothes and some makeup and stuff because we're staying at the Ho-Chunk Casino tonight."

"What?" Phoebe exclaimed. "You're kidding me."

"Nope. I figured we could stop there on our way home and have a little fun. I reserved a great room and we can try our luck at the tables. And, how about we partake of the all-you-can-eat breakfast buffet in the morning?"

Phoebe smiled at her sister. "Partake, you say?"

"Yes. Partake."

"You always surprise me. Thanks, Fran."

Fran pulled her car into a Quik Trip parking lot and threw it in park. "What the hell is with all this traffic at this time of night?"

"I have no idea," Phoebe said, looking at all the cars parked outside the gas station. "I need to pee. How about you?"

"I'm good for now."

"I'll ask around and see if something is going on around here." Phoebe exited the car and ran into the building. She walked over to the check-out clerk and whispered, "Bathroom?"

The clerk motioned to her right.

"Thanks."

A few moments later, Phoebe was picking out some chips and candy bars. She grabbed a couple of cans of Coke and stepped behind the last person in the check-out line. "Is it always this busy up here?" she asked the man standing in front of her.

He turned to look at her and smiled. "It's pretty busy up in this area all year long. A lot of vacation places, you know. The fishing can be pretty good, you know. And, then there are all those water parks that people visit all year long. Yep, pretty busy, you know."

"I didn't know that," Phoebe said, holding back a grin.

"Where are you headed?" he asked.

"We're on our way to Ho-Chunk."

"Like to do a little gambling, do you?"

"Only a little," Phoebe replied.

"I don't throw my money away gambling, you know. I worked too hard for it."

"We don't spend much," Phoebe said. "You're next."

"What?"

"You're next to check out," Phoebe told him.

"Oh, thanks."

Phoebe waited until the man paid for his items and left. She placed her items on the counter.

"Is that all?" the clerk asked her.

"That's it."

"I heard you talking to Charlie there," the clerk said. "It isn't always this busy up here this time of year but this is the week of the gun hunt for disabled sponsors. We have a lot of deer hunters up here now, so watch out for deer crossing the road."

"I will. Thanks." Phoebe finished paying for her items and turned to leave.

"Drive safe," the clerk called after her.

Phoebe turned and looked back at the woman. "I'm just curious," she said, "but where do all these hunters stay when they're up here?"

"Oh, a lot of them are local and they just go home when it gets dark. Some get motel rooms or camp out in RVs or put a tent up in the woods and sleep there. They're all over the place."

"Interesting," Phoebe said. "Thanks."

Phoebe put the bag in the back seat and slammed the door shut. She opened the front passenger door and got in. "Houston, I think we may have a problem."

"Oh, God," Fran exclaimed. "Now what?"

"There is a very good possibility that we may run into hunters camped in the woods waiting to shoot some poor helpless deer at the break of dawn."

"Ah, crap," Fran muttered. "Seriously?"

"Yep. Or, perhaps, we'll get lucky and just hit a deer."

"How long were you in there?" Fran asked.

"Too long." Phoebe laid her head back, thinking. "Any ideas?" she finally asked.

"Castle Rock Lake," Fran said. "We don't have to dump him in the lake, though. There are gobs of side roads up there and I know the area. Let's try that."

"It's almost eleven. It will probably be after one before we get to the casino."

"Probably even later," Fran replied. "We can crash there and leave in the morning."

"Maybe you should call and tell them we'll be a late arrival so they don't give our room away."

"Good idea."

"No gambling?" Phoebe asked.

"Nope. It's gonna be too late."

"Okay, but I'm not leaving until after we have partaken of the buffet in the morning," Phoebe declared, grinning.

"Partaken?"

"That's right. Look it up."

CHAPTER NINE

"Do you hear something?" Fran whispered.

Phoebe stopped walking and listened. "Just night sounds. Why? What did you hear?"

"I thought I heard a car."

"We're pretty far off the road, Fran," Phoebe said softly. "I doubt you could hear a car from here."

Fran laughed nervously. "I guess. It's probably just nerves. Let's rest for a minute."

They dropped the black lawn bag and took a few deep breaths. "I think we're far enough into the woods. Why don't we just toss him over there and head back?" Phoebe said.

"Maybe we should go a little farther," Fran replied.

"And, maybe we don't have to. Let's just go. I'm tired. I'm dirty. I'm hungry. I've had enough of this crap."

Fran thought for a moment. "Okay, don't get angry. I'm tired, too. But we shouldn't get sloppy or make any mistakes. It looks like there's a pretty heavily wooded area to our right. Let's check it out."

"How the hell can you see that? It's pitch dark out. I can barely see my hand in front of my face."

"I have eyes like a cat." Fran brushed away a small branch with leaves hanging from a tree in front of her and started walking away. "You stay here," she told Phoebe. "I'll check it out."

Phoebe watched Fran disappear into the darkness, hoping that this would be the spot. She looked around, but could barely make out anything. "Where are you?" she whispered loudly.

"Right behind you," Fran answered, making Phoebe jump.

"You jerk. You scared the shit out of me."

"Come on. Let's move him. It's a good spot with plenty of high bushes. I doubt anyone will ever find him here."

The sisters grabbed the bag and carried it over to the hiding place. "Thank goodness, that's the last one," Fran declared, as they threw the bag into the bushes. "Let's get the hell out of here."

"Which way?" Phoebe asked.

"The way we came."

"Which is what way? I don't know how we got here. My God, Fran. I think we're lost," she said, starting to panic.

"Stop it! We're not lost. Just follow me."

Fran pulled the car over and turned off the ignition. She reached over and shook Phoebe's arm. "Let's go."

Phoebe opened her eyes and looked around. "What?"

"We have one last thing to do. Remember?"

"What time is it?"

"It's almost two. We're running way behind schedule."

"Can't we do it later? Let's just go to the motel and get some rest," Phoebe whined.

"Now, Pheebs. I want it out of the car."

"All right." Phoebe opened her car door and got out. "God, I'm stiff," she declared as she stretched. "It's really gotten cold out," she declared, shivering.

Fran walked to the trunk of the car, opened it, and pulled out a black lawn bag. "Let's get changed," she told Phoebe. "Put everything you're wearing in the bag."

"Would you hand me the can of gas?" she asked Phoebe, as she threw the bag into the ditch.

"You gonna do it here?" Phoebe asked.

"Why? You don't think I should?"

"It's just that someone might drive by and see us."

"No one is going to drive by at this time of night. Now give me the gas." She reached out and took the can from Phoebe, opened it, and drenched the bag. "That's all of it," she said, as she threw the empty can on top of the bag. "Hand me the matches."

Phoebe looked confused. "I don't have any. I didn't bring any matches."

Fran stared at her. "You what? I told you to bring matches. What the hell do you think we're going to use to set that bag on fire, you idiot?"

"Don't call me an idiot."

"For crying out loud, Pheebs, can't you do anything right?"

"Stop yelling at me. I'm sorry, but I don't recall you telling me to bring any fucking matches."

"Well, I did."

"You think you did, but you didn't."

"Check the glove compartment. Maybe, there's some in there."

"Will a lighter do?" Phoebe called out after a couple of minutes.

Fran looked at her in amazement. "Unbelievable."

"Well?"

"Does it work?" Fran asked.

Phoebe gave it a couple of tries before it ignited. "Yes!" she exclaimed. She handed the lighter to Fran. "It works."

"I saw," Fran replied. "There are some paper napkins in the glove compartment. Give me a couple."

Fran took the napkins, started them on fire, and threw them on top of the bag. It ignited in one big swoosh, immediately melting the plastic bag. Fran stepped back and watched as the bag and its contents were quickly destroyed. As soon as she was satisfied nothing was left but a burned-out gas can and some ashes, she walked back to the car and got in.

"All gone?" Phoebe asked her.

"All gone."

"That was smart of you, Fran. Burning everything here instead of just throwing it all in a garbage bin at home."

"Better safe than sorry. I just hope we didn't overlook anything."

"We wore gloves the whole time," Phoebe said. "All the rags we used and the masks we wore were in there. There's no way our fingerprints can be on any of those bags we dumped."

"Let's hope." Fran turned the car around and headed back toward the freeway. "We're only about twenty minutes away from the motel. At least we'll get some sleep."

"I'm really hungry. Maybe there's a coffee shop or something open at the motel where we can get a bite to eat after we check in."

Fran smiled. "I swear I don't understand why you don't weigh two hundred pounds. Anyway, you can eat if you want, but I can't wait to hit that bed."

"I guess I take after mom. She never put weight on either."

"Well, I feel like I just lost a thousand pounds now that this is over and done with. Thank God."

"Except for one thing," Phoebe commented.

"What's that"

"We still have to find that fucking finger."

CHAPTER TEN

Thursday, November 4th

"Are you sure he was dead?" Phoebe asked as she stared at the empty couch.

"You're the one who said he was dead," Fran retorted.

"Well, maybe I was wrong. But, if I remember correctly, you agreed with me. You checked him out, too. Remember? And, if we both are wrong and he isn't dead, where is he now?" Phoebe picked up the afghan and shook it.

"Seriously? You think he's hiding in there?"

"Of course not." Phoebe sat down across from Fran and closed her eyes. "Okay, let's review. You were on the couch. He fell asleep next to you. You woke up. He didn't. He was dead. We made plans to bury him. You left him covered up on the couch. He was there when we left. And, now he isn't." She glanced at Fran. "You're the smart one. You figure it out."

"First of all, you were the one on the couch with Sammy next to you. He was sleeping or so we thought. I wasn't sleeping. Neither of us was sleeping. You discovered he was dead, not me. You have everything mixed up."

57

"So what? Dead is dead and he was dead."

Fran glared at her. "There are days I'd like to just slap you up alongside your head."

Phoebe met her gaze and held it. "Really? I don't think that's a good idea, Fran."

"I can take you. You don't have any muscle at all."

"I've got more muscle than you do," Phoebe yelled.

"Do not," Fran yelled louder. She started to get up off the couch, stopped, and stared at Phoebe. "That's the doorbell."

"See how smart you are? You know that the doorbell rang. You should get an A+ for being so smart."

"And, you should get a D- for being a dorkhead." Fran glanced over at the door as the bell rang again. "Who do you think that is?"

"Why don't you answer it and find out? They must know we are here, with you yelling so loud."

Fran gave her a dirty look. "God, I hate you."

"Good. I hate you more. Are you going to answer the door or not?"

Fran stood up and walked over to the door. She opened it a crack to see who was there. Her heart jumped.

"Ms. Figg?"

"Yes?"

"I'm Detective Handy. I wonder if I could have a few minutes of your time?"

"What's this about?"

"Do you mind if I come in?"

Fran glanced behind her to check out Phoebe, who was nowhere to be seen. She looked at the detective and smiled. "Please, come on in."

Detective Handy stepped into the house and looked around. "Nice place you have here." He sniffed the air and frowned, puzzled by the smell.

"Thank you. Please. Sit." Fran waited until Handy sat down on the couch before she sat down across from him. "So, what can I help you with, Detective?"

Handy settled on the couch and pulled out a small black notebook. "I understand you know Pastor Swinger. Is that correct?"

"Of course. He is the head pastor of our church. Why? Is something wrong with him?"

"He seems to have gone missing."

"Really?" Fran said, acting concerned. She thought for a second. "Well, I wondered what was going on. A policeman was here a few days ago asking about him. I guess his car was parked across the street for a few days."

"That's correct. So far, we haven't been able to locate him. We're hoping there's nothing wrong, but his family is starting to get worried."

"I hope he's okay," Fran declared. "He's such a nice man. My mother died recently and he was such a comfort to my family."

"So, you didn't see him the day he disappeared?"

"That was Halloween. Right?"

"Right."

"No, I'm sorry. I haven't seen him since… I guess it's been since the funeral."

Handy sniffed the air again.

"Is something wrong?" Fran asked.

"I'm trying to figure out what that smell is," he said.

"Oh, my. Does my house smell bad?" Fran asked, looking concerned. "I'm so sorry." She smelled the air. "I don't smell anything," she said, looking confused.

"I'm sure it's nothing," Handy said. "Do you live here alone, Ms. Figg?"

"My sister, Phoebe, lives with me," Fran told him.

"Is she around? I'd like to speak to her if I could."

Fran shook her head no. "I'm sorry. I have no idea where she is, but I'll tell her you stopped by." Fran stood up, making it clear she was ready for the detective to leave. "Oh!" she exclaimed.

"What is it?"

"You must be smelling bleach. Is that it?"

Detective Handy hesitated. "It just might be," he finally replied.

"My cat died a couple of days ago. Unfortunately, he made a mess... Well, you know what I mean." She turned away, her eyes filling with tears. "I loved him so much," she sniveled.

"I'm so sorry," Handy said, walking toward the door.

"It was all over the kitchen and living room and I thought I'd..."

"I get it," Handy said. "It's the bleach for sure." He opened the door and turned.

"I guess I just don't smell it anymore. I better get some air fresheners..."

"Thank you for your help," Handy said, interrupting her, as he pulled the door shut behind him. He stood on the small porch and took a deep breath. "Crazy women and their cats," he mumbled.

Fran stood in front of the window smiling. "Well, he won't be back anytime soon," she uttered to herself.

"You're quite the actress."

Fran turned and grinned. "I guess. You sure disappeared in a hurry."

"And, aren't you glad I did?"

"I am. You being questioned by a cop spells nothing but disaster."

"He thought it stinks in here, Fran. What do you think he smells? I don't smell anything anymore. I think I'm immune to it."

"It has to be a combination of bleach, baking soda, and vinegar. I'm surprised that we aren't dead, inhaling all that shit," Fran said.

"Plus, that Smelleze. That's some powerful stuff, too."

"Well, at least we don't smell rotting flesh anymore."

"I wonder what we can use to cover up all the stuff we've used to cover up the stench of death."

"Stench of death?" Fran repeated, grinning.

"Well, what would you call it?"

"I'll pick up a boatload full of air fresheners tomorrow. Maybe one of those will do the job."

"We can only hope. In the meanwhile, let's open some windows and air this place out," Phoebe suggested.

"It's freezing out," Fran said.

"All the better."

"I'm sorry about before," Fran told her.

"Me, too. We shouldn't fight with each other."

"All's good, then?" Fran asked.

"All's good," Phoebe replied.

Fran walked over to the couch and sat down. "Pheebs, what do you think happened to Sammy?" she asked after a few moments.

Phoebe shook her head. "I haven't a clue but we better find him and that finger or..."

"Or, what?"

Phoebe sighed as she looked at her sister. "All I know is that we better find Sammy and that finger and I'm betting that the two are in the same place."

"I told you before; you're not cutting Sammy open," Fran exclaimed.

"Then, you better find that finger fast, because if I find Sammy before you find that finger..."

"What?"

"Chop, chop, Big Sister."

CHAPTER ELEVEN

"That 'chop, chop' statement was out of line, you know," Fran said as she took a bite of pizza.

"I know and I'm sorry. But until I know where the hell Sammy and that finger are, I'm gonna be a nervous wreck."

"We've got the weekend to figure it out, Sis. It's back to work on Monday."

"For you, anyway," Phoebe said. "I don't think I'm ever going to find a job."

"Of course, you will. Just don't give up. I'm sure someone out there is looking for help."

"Well, if they are, they sure aren't looking my way. I'm so tired of being turned down after every interview I have."

"Just hang in there, Kiddo," Fran said encouragingly. "Something is bound to come up soon."

"I guess," Phoebe said sighing. She looked at the pizza box in the middle of the table. "Do you want the last piece?" she asked Fran.

Fran smiled. "I'm full. You can have it." She waited for Phoebe to take the last piece, picked up the box the pizza came in, and closed it up. "I'll toss this. You want to put the plates in the dishwasher when you're done?"

"Sure."

"What do you want to do tonight?"

"I'm tired, Fran. I think I'll just crawl into bed and call it a day.

As Swinger turned to see who Phoebe was yelling at, she bucked her body throwing him to the side of her. She rolled away from him, jumped up, and ran out of the kitchen, heading for the front door. As she glanced behind her, she was shocked to see that he was only a few feet away. Knowing she would never get the door open in time, she ran for the stairs. He was fat, but he was fast. She almost made it to the top stair before he grabbed her hair and yanked, stopping her in her tracks.

"Whoa, there. I'm not done with you."

Phoebe tried to pull away, but the harder she fought the harder he pulled. "Let go of me, you prick," she screamed.

"Which room is yours?"

She managed to turn slightly and swung a fist at his face. Swinger took a step back and she missed, only to wind up facing him. "Let me go."

He slapped her hard with his free hand, knocking her to the floor. "Get up," he shouted.

Phoebe went limp. He grabbed the back of her top and pulled her through the first door at the top of the stairs; her dead mother's bedroom. He dropped her on the floor and looked around the room, remembering that he had been here before. This is where he visited Fran and Phoebe's mother before she passed away. This is where he held the woman's hand and prayed with her. He grinned. And, now, this is where he was going to get his rocks off with her daughter.

Phoebe opened her eyes and stared at Swinger. "Why?" she sobbed. "Why are you doing this?"

"Get on the bed," Swinger said. "Now!"

Phoebe didn't move. "Just go. I won't say anything. I promise."

"Nobody would believe you if you did say anything. I'm a minister. I'm a man of God and you're nothing. Just like your mother was nothing."

"I don't understand. What did we ever do to you?"

"Oh, not you. It was your mother, thinking she was too good for me. I asked her to marry me, you know. She laughed at me. I may not have screwed your mother, but by the time I get done with you..." He looked down at his crotch. "Freddy's all excited," he exclaimed. "See."

Phoebe looked shocked. "You asked my mother to marry you? No, you didn't. She would have said something."

"Maybe, you didn't know your whore mother as well as you thought you did. She was a tease. She was what we call a prick-teaser."

"No way," Phoebe yelled. "You're lying."

"Get on the bed. Now!"

"No!"

Swinger reached down, picked her up, and threw her face down on her mother's bed. He pulled his pants down, his erection standing proud and ready. As Phoebe tried to roll over onto her back, he grabbed her pants and pulled them down to her knees.

"Stop it," she yelled.

"Spread your legs," he demanded.

"Please, no," Phoebe begged, sobbing now. "Don't do this."

Swinger grabbed her legs and tried to spread them. Realizing he was limited, due to her pants being down around her knees, he grabbed her pants again and yanked them down to her ankles. "That's better," he mumbled.

Phoebe, crying hysterically now, tried to roll to her side, but Swinger simply put his hands on her back and held her in place. "Ready? Here comes Freddy!" he exclaimed, laughing loudly.

Phoebe shut her eyes and held her breath.

"Phoebe, wake up."

Phoebe jumped. "No, don't," she cried out.

Fran gently pushed the hair away from Phoebe's face. "Wake up. You were having a nightmare."

Phoebe opened her eyes and shuddered. "I was dreaming," she stated.

"Yes," Fran agreed.

"Will they ever stop?" Phoebe asked. "Will these horrible dreams ever come to an end?"

"I hope so, Pheebs."

"You don't have them, do you? How come you don't have bad dreams?"

"I don't know. Maybe I'm still in denial."

Phoebe sat up and smiled. "I hope you never get them. It's horrible."

"Well, you went through a lot, Pheebs. No one should have to go through what you did."

"Did mom ever talk to you about Swinger?"

"We've talked about this already. She never said anything to me about him or his advances."

"He was lying, wasn't he?"

"Of course, he was. You have to forget everything he said. Everything! Understand?"

"Easy for you to say," Phoebe said grinning.

"One other thing, Pheebs."

"What's that?"

"It may not be a good idea to eat right before you go to bed. I've heard that can bring on bad dreams."

"No way. I've never heard that."

"Google it tomorrow. But I'll bet you anything that it's true."

"Thanks, Fran."

"You're welcome. I'll see you in the morning."

"Not if I see you first."

CHAPTER TWELVE

<u>Friday, November 5th</u>

"Who the hell is ringing our doorbell this early in the morning?" Phoebe exclaimed as she walked out of her bedroom. "Fran?"

"I hear it."

"Should I answer it?"

"Yeah. I'll be down in a minute."

Phoebe closed her robe as she ran down the stairs. The doorbell rang again. "All right," she yelled. "I'm coming." She opened the door. "What is..." She looked surprised. "Gary. What are you doing here? We didn't expect you to be back already."

"Yet, here I am, Pheebs. Where's my girl?"

"Come on in."

"Who is it, Pheebs?" Fran called out as she started down the stairs.

"Surprise!"

Fran looked toward the door and let out a screech. "Oh, my God, Gary." She ran toward his outstretched arms. "I didn't expect you until next week."

Gary pulled her close and kissed her. "We finished up and I got an earlier flight."

"I'm going back to bed," Phoebe said. "This is the last thing I need to watch this morning."

"Oh, shush," Fran said. "Be a good girl and go put on a pot of coffee, will you?"

"What smells?" Gary asked, sniffing the air.

Fran glanced over at Phoebe, shaking her head ever so slightly. "Bleach. Pheebs and I have been on a cleaning spree the past few days."

"Talking about the past few days, my love..."

"Yes?" Fran said.

"Where were you two the other night?"

"What do you mean?"

"I stopped by to surprise you and the house was empty."

"Yesterday? We were home yesterday, weren't we, Pheebs?"

"No. I mean on Thursday," Gary said.

"You were back already on Thursday? How come you waited until now to see me?"

"Actually, I got back on Wednesday," Gary explained. "I had a lot of paperwork to finish up, so I didn't get a chance to come over until Thursday night."

"Why didn't you come over yesterday?" Fran asked.

"I had meetings all day with 'the boss', which extended into a late night of drinking. A lot of drinking." He pulled Fran close and hugged her. "But, I'm here now, Baby, and I'm all yours."

Phoebe realized she was holding her breath and slowly let it out. She turned and walked into the kitchen. As she went to pick up the coffee pot, she noticed that her hands were shaking. "Get hold of yourself," she mumbled.

Fran and Gary walked into the kitchen, holding hands and smiling. "I'm making breakfast," Fran declared. "Do you want anything?"

"You two look happy," Phoebe said smiling. "No thanks; I'll pass. I think I'll take a shower, get dressed, and go do a little shopping. I could use a few new things for my job interviews."

"Still no job?" Gary asked her.

"Nope. I just can't understand why nobody wants to hire someone who is good at doing nothing."

"Ah, come on. That's not true," Gary told her.

"Really? And, just what am I good at, may I ask?"

"Obviously, you're good at emptying bleach bottles. My, God, how many bottles did you two go through? I can't believe the house was that dirty?"

Fran laughed. "Of course, it wasn't. But, Phoebe, as you well know, is a klutz. She knocked a bottle over and it got on everything. Right, Pheebs?"

Phoebe grinned. "That's me all right. Just a big klutz." She poured water into the coffee maker and hit the on switch. "It should be ready in a few," she said, as she walked toward the door.

"Wait a minute," Gary told her.

Phoebe turned and looked at him. "What?"

"Sit down for a minute, will you?" He glanced over at Fran. "You, too, Honey."

"What is it?" Fran inquired. 'You're making me nervous."

"It's about Sammy," Gary said seriously. "Haven't you missed him?"

"Of course, I've missed him. Why? Do you know where he is?" Fran asked hesitantly.

"I'm sorry, Fran, but he's dead."

70

Phoebe stared at Fran, waiting to see her reaction.

"What do... I mean, how do you..."

"Oh, for crying out loud, Fran, spit it out," Phoebe said loudly. She glanced up at Gary. "What do you mean, he's dead? We thought he took off."

"Where is he?" Fran asked Gary, tears welling up in the corner of her eyes. "What makes you think my Sammy is dead?" She reached for a napkin as she started to cry.

"Well, he better be dead, because I buried him," Gary said.

"What the hell are you talking about?" Phoebe asked him, looking confused. "We were gone for a short time and when we got home, he was missing. How could you have buried him?"

"When I came over, you weren't here so I let myself in with the key you gave me. Remember?" he asked, looking at Fran.

"I remember."

"Anyway, he was on the couch. I thought he was sleeping but when I reached down to pet him, he was dead as a doornail. And, stiff. Damn, he was really stiff. I waited a while for you to show up, but when you didn't, I decided to bury him. You know? So, you wouldn't have to deal with it."

"Why didn't you call me?" Fran asked. "You should have called and told me."

"I guess, but – well, I wasn't thinking that way, you know. I still wanted to surprise you, so I just buried him and left."

"You dumb ass!" Phoebe yelled. "Here we have been worried sick about Sammy and looking all over for him

71

and all this time he's buried..." She stopped and looked at Gary. "Where did you bury him? Where is he?"

"In the backyard," he said softly. "I was gonna make a little cross for his grave. If that's all right with you, Fran."

Fran wiped her eyes and shook her head. "That's fine."

"I'm sorry. Really, I am," Gary said. "I handled this all wrong. But I didn't know where you were and I didn't want to leave him on the couch for you to find him like that."

Fran reached over and took Gary's hand. "It's fine. It really is. Thank you for taking care of it for me." She glanced over at the coffee pot and stood up. "Coffee's ready."

"I'll have mine later. I'm gonna go shower," Phoebe said, as she left the room.

"She is so pissed," Gary declared.

"Well, we have spent a lot of time looking for him," Fran said, tears running down her cheeks.

"I'll talk to her," Gary said.

"Just give her some time to cool off. So, show me," Fran said.

"Show you what?" Gary asked her.

"Where you buried Sammy. I want to see where he is."

"I'll show you later, Honey. How about right now you take me upstairs and give me a proper welcome home." Gary grabbed Fran, pulled her onto his lap, and kissed her.

Phoebe dressed in a pair of old jeans and a sweatshirt. She pulled on a pair of old boots and ran downstairs. "I'll see you later," she yelled, as she put on her jacket and hurried out the kitchen door to the backyard. She looked around for a recently dug cat grave. "Where the hell is it?" she uttered. She started walking the perimeter of the backyard and stopped. "There you are," she whispered as she turned and went into the garage.

Ten minutes later the empty hole was filled in. Phoebe put the shovel back in the garage, carefully placed the box in a garbage bag, tightly closed it, and put the bag in the trunk of her car. "Chop, chop, Sister," she muttered, smiling as she drove away. "Chop, chop."

CHAPTER THIRTEEN

"Man, I've missed you," Gary exclaimed, as he rolled over onto his back, trying to catch his breath.

Fran grinned. "Obviously. I must say that was quite something."

"I try."

"I'm glad you do." She laid her head back on her pillow and closed her eyes. "I'm so glad you're back home," she said. "It's been rough since mom died. And, Pheebs... Well, you know she can be a handful at times."

"Don't you think it's about time you quit trying to be her mother? She's a grown woman, Fran, and she needs to start taking responsibility for her life. She's never going to grow up if you don't quit treating her like a little kid."

"I know. As soon as she gets a job, I'm..."

"You mean if she gets a job," Gary interrupted. "She's been looking for work ever since I met you. Are you sure she's even going on all those interviews?"

"Why would you say that?" Fran asked, raising her voice. "Pheebs wouldn't lie to me."

"Maybe not. But it seems to me that somebody should have hired her by now. My God, she can't even get a job as a waitress."

"You know what, Gary? Waitressing is hard work and you need a good head for that. I don't care for the way you're talking about her," Fran said loudly.

"Don't get mad. I didn't mean anything by that. I like Phoebe. You know that. I just think that it takes a lot out of you, having to take care of her."

"I don't take care of her, Gary. I watch out for her. There is a difference, you know."

"I know. You're a good woman, Fran." He reached over and pulled her close. "I'm lucky to have you."

Phoebe was standing at the bottom of the stairs listening to her sister and Gary talk. "That fucker," Phoebe said under her breath. She walked over to the front door, opened it, and slammed it shut. "I'm home," she yelled. "Where are you guys?"

"We'll be down in a few minutes," Fran shouted.

Phoebe took her coat off and hung it up. She grabbed the remote, turned on the television, and plopped down onto a comfortable overstuffed chair. She started channel surfing and finally settled on the History Channel. After a few minutes, she put her head back and closed her eyes.

"No, no, no. Please, no."

"That's good. Beg some more. Maybe, I'll stop," Swinger teased. *"I'm getting close now,"* he said, laughing. *"Freddy is more than ready."*

"I'm begging you. Please stop."

"What will you do if I stop? What will you give me, Mary?"

"What's wrong with you? I'm not Mary."

"Get away from my sister!"

As Swinger turned to look behind him, a red steel knitting needle entered his left ear, proceeded through his eardrum, and entered his brain. He opened his mouth to scream but all that emerged was a soft squeak as he died and fell backward onto the floor.

"Are you okay?" Fran asked Phoebe.

Phoebe rolled over and stared at her sister, sobbing hysterically. "He was... he...he tried to..."

Fran went over to her and held her as you would a small child. "I know. I know," she said softly. She rocked Phoebe back and forth as Phoebe cried. Slowly, the sobs subsided and Phoebe settled down. Phoebe sat back and gazed at Fran. "You saved me," she stated. "He was going to rape me and you saved me."

"Are you okay?" Fran asked again.

Phoebe shook her head yes. "I guess. He called me Mary."

"I heard that."

"He thought I was mom. He had to be crazy, don't you think?"

"I think that anyone who tries what he just tried, has to be off their rocker."

Phoebe took a deep breath. "Why are you home?" she asked, looking confused. "You said you were going to trick and treat with Deanna and her kids."

"I was. But her husband came home early from work and I decided not to tag along, so I came home."

"Oh, thank God you did." Phoebe hugged Fran. "Thank you."

Fran walked around the bed and looked down at Swinger. "God, he really is a fat fuck, isn't he?"

"Is he dead?" Phoebe asked.

"Oh, he's dead, all right," Fran told her, laughing sarcastically.

Phoebe stood up and sat right back down. "My legs are shaking so bad; I can't even stand."

"Well, at least pull your pants up, will you?"

"I guess we better call the police," Phoebe declared.

"Wait. Let's think about this for a minute," Fran said.

"What's there to think about? The bastard tried to rape me."

"A minister tried to rape you."

"So?"

"A well-respected member of the community, who is loved by everyone who knows him, tried to rape you."

"What are you getting at?" Phoebe asked.

"Everyone knows you're a flirt. Who's going to believe that he tried to rape you? Even if you went to a doctor right now, there's no proof that he did anything."

"So, it's my fault? Is that what you're saying?"

"Of course not. I know it's not your fault. But that isn't what the police are going to think. Why was he here? Why did you let him in? No, Pheebs, I don't think calling the cops is a good idea."

"What do you suggest we do? In case you didn't notice, there's a dead body on the floor and you killed him."

"To save you from being raped."

"And, I appreciate it. But you didn't have to kill him. You could have hit him over the head with something and knocked him out."

"My only thought was to help you, Pheebs. I didn't care how. God, I can't believe you're upset because he's dead. I guess I should have let him go at you."

"I'm sorry. I didn't mean it that way. Of course, I'm glad you..." Phoebe teared up. "I'm sorry. I'm going to shower."

"He isn't bleeding that much. Let's put something under his head to catch the blood."

"I said I was going to go shower."

"I heard you. First, though, we need to figure out what to do with him."

"I vote we call the police," Phoebe told her.

"I vote no. If we do and it doesn't go well, I could end up in prison for murder and you probably would too."

"I didn't do anything," Phoebe cried out. "I was the one he was trying to rape."

"In the least, you'd be considered an accessory to murder. We could both go to jail, Pheebs." Fran turned and walked out of the room.

"Where are you going?" Phoebe called after her.

"Downstairs to get some towels to soak up this blood."

"Fran, this isn't right. We can't do this."

"I think we can," Fran said.

"While you're down there, turn the oven off, will you?" Phoebe yelled.

"Will do," Fran answered, shouting.

Phoebe stood over Swinger's body and spit. She glanced at his crotch and was surprised to see that he still had an erection. "Huh. Well, look at that. It looks like he's going to hell with a hard-on," she mumbled.

"Do you mind if we change the channel?" Fran asked.

Phoebe opened her eyes and blinked a few times. "Sorry, I guess I dozed off. What did you say?"

"The remote, please," Fran said, holding out her hand.

Phoebe handed her the remote and yawned. "What's for dinner?"

Fran shrugged. 'I don't know. I guess we can order something."

"Where's Gary?"

"Taking a shower. He should be down in a minute."

Fran sat down on the couch and smiled. "It sure is nice having him back."

"How long will he be here this time?"

"I don't know. We haven't talked about it yet." Fran glanced toward the stairs. "Feel better?" she asked Gary.

"I feel great." He sat down on the cushion next to her and grinned. "Thanks to you." He reached over and kissed her.

"Gross," Phoebe said making a face. "Turn it off for a while, will you?"

Gary laughed. "You're just jealous."

As Phoebe watched them, she noticed something sticking out between two of the cushions. As the cushions sunk deeper due to Gary's and Fran's weight, the object became more pronounced. Phoebe's heart started to pound.

"What are you staring at?" Fran asked.

"Nothing," Phoebe replied, as she felt herself getting warmer by the second. "It's just..."

"What's the matter?" Gary asked.

"I don't know. I feel really hot like I'm going to faint or something." She felt her forehead. "I'm really warm. I think I need... Gary, would you get me a glass of water, please."

"Of course." Gary jumped off the couch and hurried into the kitchen.

"What's wrong with you?" Fran asked.

"The finger."

"What?"

"The finger," Phoebe said again, as she pointed to the space between the cushions.

Fran glanced down and jumped back. She glanced toward the kitchen. "What should I do? Gary will be here in a minute."

"Sit on it"

"What?"

"Sit on it. Well, you can't pick it up," Phoebe whispered.

Fran looked at the finger again. "It's all gross. I'm not going to sit on it."

"Here you go," Gary said, as he walked back into the living room and handed Phoebe a glass of water.

"Thank you." Phoebe took a long swallow. "That's better."

"You okay now?" Gary asked.

"I'm fine. Well, not really. I think my blood sugar may be a little low. Would you mind getting me a cookie?"

"I guess," he said, getting a little aggravated. "Where are they?"

"In the cabinet over the stove."

"I'll be right back. Don't go passing out now," Gary told her.

"Thanks."

"Do something. Get it out of there," Phoebe whispered to Fran as Gary walked back to the kitchen.

Fran looked around trying to find something to use to pick the finger up. "With what?" she asked.

"Oh, for crying out loud," Phoebe said disgusted with her sister. She reached into her pocket, pulled out a Kleenex, wrapped it over the top of the finger, and pulled. She barely held back a shriek, as the tip of the finger slid away, leaving the white bone protruding from the gap between the cushions. She dropped the Kleenex onto the floor and stepped back.

"Pick it up," Fran whispered.

"I'm not gonna pick it up. You pick it up," Phoebe replied

"Pick what up?" Gary asked as he walked in from the kitchen, carrying a tin of cookies in one hand and a glass of milk in the other.

CHAPTER FOURTEEN

"I think we just found a dead mouse," Fran exclaimed, jumping up off the couch. She looked at the object on the floor and shuddered. "Sammy must have brought it in."

Phoebe stood up, turned quickly, bumped the edge of her chair, and lost her balance. She fell forward into Gary who dropped the glass, causing the milk to spill onto the carpet. "I'm sorry, Gary. Did any get on you?"

Gary looked down at his khaki slacks and frowned. "Looks like it did. Shit! Now my pants are going to stink from that milk," he replied, trying to hold his temper.

"Come with me," Fran said. "I'll help you clean them." She glanced at Phoebe. "Pick up that glass, will you?"

"I'm sorry," Phoebe told her. "It was an accident."

"Come on, Gary. Let's go into the kitchen."

Phoebe waited until Fran and Gary were in the kitchen, then reached down and picked the glass up from off the floor. She grabbed the Kleenex and tossed it into the glass. She looked at the bone protruding from between the two cushions and made a sour face. She set the glass down and walked into the kitchen.

"How you doing?" she asked.

"Fine, Pheebs. We're doing just fine."

"Good. I need some paper towels to clean up the milk. Do we have any carpet cleaner?"

"In the pantry."

"Are there paper towels in there, too?"

"There are some right here on the counter. You can use them."

"They're almost gone. I'll open a new roll." Phoebe opened the pantry door and took out a roll of paper towels." She looked around. "I don't see the carpet cleaner stuff," she told Fran.

"Second shelf on the right."

"Oh, here it is. Thanks." Phoebe smiled at Fran as she walked back into the living room. She pulled a couple of towels off the roll and dropped them over the glass. Reaching down, she turned the glass upside down so the skin wrapped in the tissue would fall onto the towels. She crunched the towel up, making sure the skin couldn't fall out.

Pulling a couple more towels off the roll, she wrapped them around the finger between the cushions and pulled. It broke off at the first joint. "Shit!" she exclaimed.

"Now what?" Gary asked as he walked back into the living room. "What are you doing? I thought you were going to clean up this mess you made."

"I am. I wanted to make sure there wasn't any part of that mouse left on the couch." She picked up the roll of towels and threw them to him. "Here, make yourself useful. I'm gonna toss this mouse in the garbage outside." She picked up the towels from the floor and grabbed the glass.

"Pheebs, can you come in here for a minute?" Fran called from the kitchen.

"On my way," Phoebes yelled. "Excuse me a minute, will you, Gary?" she asked as she walked past him.

"Nice move in there, Pheebs. Pretending to trip."

"Thanks."

"Did you clean it up? Fran inquired.

"Done. Well, almost anyway."

"What do you mean almost?"

"Part of the finger is still stuck between the cushions. But you can't see it anymore."

Fran closed her eyes, took a deep breath, and let it out. "Part? What do you mean, part?"

"It broke when I was pulling it out and then your dumb boyfriend came back in the room and I didn't have time to fish the rest out."

"His name is Gary. Don't call him dumb."

"I'll call him whatever I feel like calling him. I don't like him."

"Just get your act together, will you?"

"I have some good news," Phoebe told her, smiling as she changed the subject.

"That would be a nice change. What is it?"

"I'm not gonna have to cut Sammy open."

"Of course, you're not going to cut him open," Fran agreed. "Besides, he's buried."

"Well, he was buried. Now he's not."

Fran grabbed the back of a chair and steadied herself. "What did you do, Pheebs?"

"I dug him up."

Fran pulled the chair out and sat down. "I swear, you're gonna be the death of me."

"I told you if we didn't find that finger, I was going to cut him open. Well, we found the finger. I would think you would be happy that he'll be buried in one piece. Or reburied, I should say," she said grinning.

"You're not funny, Pheebs. Gary, would you come in here?" Fran yelled.

"What are you doing?" Phoebe whispered.

"What is it?" Gary asked as he entered the kitchen. He threw the paper towels at Phoebe. "Catch."

"Would you please sit down?" Fran requested.

"What is it? You look upset," Gary asked, looking concerned.

"My dear, sweet, dumb sister was upset because you buried Sammy so she dug him up. She thinks we should have a proper funeral for him so we can have closure."

"You dug him up!" Gary yelled at her.

"Yes, Gary, I dug him up. He was Fran's cat, not yours. I don't think it was right for you to take it upon yourself to bury him. Fran and I had already decided that he should be buried with his favorite toy, Mousey, and maybe his blanket or pillow. I don't know, maybe all of his stuff. We'll need to get a bigger box so it all fits, of course. Could you take care of that for us? You know, find a bigger box."

"Fran?" Gary said, looking confused. "What the hell is going on? You decided? When did you decide? Did you know he was dead?"

"Of course, not. It's just that after mom died, we talked about what we would do when Sammy died. I guess we kind of planned his funeral. After all, Sammy was getting up there in years. It was only a matter of time."

He stared at Phoebe. "So, you decided to dig him up."

"That's right. Now we can give him a proper farewell."

"But, why did you fill the hole back in?"

"How do you know that?

"I was out in back having a smoke. I would have noticed if there was a hole there."

"Well, why do you think?" Phoebe replied. "The last thing we need is a lawsuit because somebody stepped in a hole and got hurt."

Gary stared at her. "Just how many people do you have running around in your backyard in November? You're a little nuts, you know."

"Well, I'd rather be nuts than be an asshole like you."

"Phoebe!" Fran yelled. "That was totally out of line. Apologize to Gary."

"I don't think so. I know what he thinks of me. I heard you guys talking. Well, he's no prize, I can tell you." She turned away and looked out the kitchen window. "Tell her, Gary, or I will. I think it's about time that Fran knows just what kind of an asshole you really are."

"Shut the fuck up, Phoebe," Gary yelled.

"What are you talking about?" Fran asked getting upset.

"Ask your boyfriend." Phoebe turned and walked out of the kitchen.

"Gary?"

"I swear I don't know what she's talking about."

"Phoebe wouldn't say that if she didn't have a reason."

"She's off her rocker. There's nothing to tell."

"Seriously?"

Gary looked away. "You know, Fran, I've had enough of this nonsense. I'm gonna go. I'll call you later. Maybe you and your sister will have this straightened out by then."

"Look at me." Gary turned toward her. Fran stared him in the eyes. "Promise me I have nothing to worry about."

Gary laughed nervously. "I promise."

"You're such a liar," Phoebe said as she walked back into the room. "He made a pass at me," she told Fran. "It was right before he left to go wherever the hell it was he went for six months. It was late and I couldn't sleep so I came downstairs to get a glass of milk. I hadn't put my robe on. Obviously, I didn't know he would be sitting at the kitchen table. He got fresh, Fran. I told him to stop, but he wouldn't."

"Gary? Is this true?" Fran asked softly.

"You little bitch. Why don't you tell her the real story?" He glanced at Fran. "It wasn't me that started it. It was her. She came on to me. I'm only human, you know. She came prancing in here wearing her see-through little baby doll pajamas, all surprised to see me she says. Before I knew what was happening, she was all over me."

"That's a rotten lie, Gary, and you know it. If mom hadn't come downstairs and stopped him, Fran, who knows what might have happened? He begged mom and me not to say anything to you. We finally agreed when he promised he would never try anything like that again. I'm so sorry, Fran. I should have told you months ago."

"It's okay, Pheebs. It's not your fault. You can't help it if men find you attractive."

"She's a fucking liar. I'll admit that I got caught up in it but I sure as hell didn't start it." Gary said, glaring at Phoebe. "I'm sorry, Fran. But it was months ago. It's history. Let's just forget about it."

"I don't know if I can." Fran walked over to the counter, opened a drawer, and took out a butcher knife.

Phoebe stared at her. "Fran, what do you..."

"It's okay, Pheebs," she interrupted, shaking her head no, as she stood behind Gary.

Gary turned and yelled, "What the hell do you think..."

"You were a bad boy, Gary," she said softly as she grabbed his hair and yanked his head back toward her. "You need to be punished."

Phoebe gasped as Fran pulled the knife across Gary's throat, slicing his jugular vein. She let go of his hair and watched his face fall forward onto the table.

"What have you done?" Phoebe screamed.

"It looks like we're going to have to buy some more of those lawn bags, Pheebs."

CHAPTER FIFTEEN

"You need to call an ambulance," Phoebe screamed. "Now!"

"I think it's too late."

"He's dead? You're sure?"

Fran poked Gary on the shoulder. "I'm pretty sure."

"Well, is he or isn't he?"

Fran walked around to the other side of the table, bent down, and stared at Gary's face. "His eyes are open," she said. "Gary?" She stood up and looked at Phoebe. "He's dead," she declared.

"I am not helping you cut up another body," Phoebe informed her sister loudly. "In fact, right now I'm seriously thinking about getting out of here and away from you. What the hell were you thinking?"

"I don't know what happened. I didn't mean to kill him. I was only going to scare him a little, that's all."

"You didn't mean to kill him?" Phoebe shouted. "What the hell do you think was going to happen when you stuck a knife in his throat?" She glanced over at Gary and turned away. "Do something, for God's sake. He's getting blood all over everything."

"What do you suggest? I don't know how to stop the bleeding."

"Well, either do I. I'm not a doctor. Towels. Get some towels and put them around his neck."

"You do it. I can't touch him."

"Now you're squeamish? Just do it, Fran."

"But what if he isn't dead?"

"Oh, he's dead, all right," Phoebe told her. "Congratulations, you've killed another one. You are now officially a serial killer."

"I can't," Fran said, her whole body shaking now. "I can't, I can't, I..." She dropped to her knees, moaning. "What did I do? My God, what did I do?"

Phoebe turned around and opened a door that led to a utility room. She picked up a large pail, some big sponges, and a stack of rags. She walked back into the kitchen and stared at Fran. "Stop it!" she yelled. "Just stop that wailing, will you?"

Fran started to cry even harder, rocking back and forth on her knees.

Phoebe threw the items she was carrying across the room. "When you're ready to pull yourself together, start cleaning up this mess. And, don't walk in the other room with those bloody shoes on."

Fran looked up and wiped her eyes. "Where are you going?"

"I'm going to move my car so I can put your dumb-ass boyfriend's car in the garage. We don't need it sitting in the driveway. We can figure out what to do with it as soon as you get this mess cleaned up."

"Aren't you going to help me clean up?" Fran whined.

"No."

"Why not? I can't do this all by myself, Pheebs."

"Because while you are cleaning up in here, I'm gonna be digging Mr. Dumb Ass a grave in the backyard. Tell me, Fran, do you want him buried with Sammy or should I dig a separate grave for him?"

"You can't dig a hole that big. You're not strong enough and the ground is frozen. You can't do that by yourself."

"The ground isn't frozen. And, I'm not cleaning up this kitchen, so I'll wait until you're done and we'll go dig the hole together. How does that sound?"

Fran started crying again. "That's not fair."

"Fair?" Phoebe yelled. "I don't think it's fair that I had to watch Gary bleed to death in our kitchen after you stuck a knife in his throat. I don't think it's fair that I had to cut up Swinger because you killed him instead of just clubbing him over his head. I don't think it's..." She stopped talking and walked over to the door that led into the living room. "Oh, to hell with it all."

"I'm sorry, but life isn't always fair," Fran declared. I don't know why I did this. Honestly, Pheebs, that wasn't my intention. Won't you help me? If we work together, we can have this cleaned up in no time. Please."

Phoebe fought to hold back the tears. "The first thing we have to do is get his body wrapped up and out of here."

Fran let out a sigh of relief. "Thank you. You're the best."

"I must be nuts to help you do this," Phoebe mumbled.

"I'll get some old sheets. We can wrap him in those. Okay?"

"We need to move him. I think we should put him in the garage for now," Phoebe suggested.

Fran looked at Gary. "I think the bleeding has stopped."

"Stopped? Hell, he hasn't got any left. It's all over the kitchen floor."

"You know, Pheebs, we could... I'm thinking that cutting Swinger up wasn't that bad. Maybe we could..."

"Don't even think about it, Fran. I'll help you get rid of his body, but there is no way in hell we are cutting him up," Phoebe interrupted. "No fucking way! Got it?"

"All right. Geez, you don't have to be so nasty."

"Get started. I'm going to move Gary's car."

Phoebe pulled her top over her head, stepped out of her jeans, and kicked off her shoes. "Let's get to it."

"Good idea. Give me a minute to take my clothes off, too."

"Why? You're already covered in blood. No reason to take them off. We'll burn them along with all the other stuff after we finish up in here. Now pick up that pail and fill it with water. We've got a long night ahead of us."

"He was a lot easier to move than Swinger, wasn't he?" Fran commented.

"Uh-huh," Phoebe mumbled.

"Of course, he probably weighed half of what Swinger weighed."

"Probably."

"Until we cut the fat ass up, that is." Fran declared.

"Whatever." Phoebe glanced over at Fran. "He didn't lose any weight, Fran. He still weighed the same."

"Even so, he was a lot easier to carry after we put him in separate bags." She waited for Phoebe to answer her. "Right?"

"Uh-huh."

Fran dipped the bloody rag she was using into the pail, swished it around in the water, twisted it, and continued to wipe down the floor. "You're not very talkative. Something biting your ass?"

"I'm trying to decide what to do. I'm supposed to pick up Cynthia and Gladys around seven-thirty. There's that baby shower for Cassi tonight. I think I should go."

"You can't go and leave me here all alone," Fran exclaimed.

"Well, I can, but that's not the point. If I don't go it will look suspicious. I already confirmed it with Gladys and they're expecting me to pick them up."

"There's still a lot of cleaning up to do, Pheebs."

"You can manage for a few hours without me. The baby shower should only last a couple of hours. I'll leave if it goes too long."

"You know it's gonna be longer than two hours," Fran whined. "I need help."

"We've already cleaned up most of the blood. There isn't that much left to do, Fran."

"Well, go party then, if that is what you want to do," Fran said angrily. "I guess I can't depend on you to help me."

"Just get over yourself, will you? If you hadn't stuck a knife in Gary, there wouldn't be a mess to clean up in the first place. And, by the way, Fran, how about coming up with a plan while I'm gone."

"A plan for what?"

"A plan to decide what we're going to do with Gary and his car. We've got to get it out of here and the sooner the better."

"I've already thought about it. I'm going to text Gary's mom and tell her that he's coming to visit for a few days."

"Okay. Then what?"

"Then, somewhere between here and Dubuque, his car crashes and starts on fire or something like that. Maybe he drives into the river and drowns. I like burning better, though. It might cover up the neck thing."

"The neck thing? You mean almost cutting his head off?"

"Don't exaggerate. It wasn't that bad. I just hit the wrong place, that's all."

"You think? I didn't know his parents lived in Dubuque. That's about a ninety-minute drive," Phoebe said, changing the subject.

"Just his mom lives there. His dad is dead. Anyway, we don't have to go all the way to Dubuque. We can do it anywhere."

"Okay." Phoebe thought for a minute. "We'll take two cars. I'll follow you. I don't want to get into Gary's car at all. I don't want my prints anywhere near it. It wouldn't be strange if your prints are found in it, though. Seeing as how you were dating."

"If we do it right, there won't be any prints left to worry about. We'll put Gary in the driver's seat, pour a couple of gallons of gas all over the car – inside and out - and light a match." She stared at Phoebe. "Just be sure you have matches this time."

"Don't start, Fran." She glanced at her watch. "I've got to clean up and get ready."

"Try to get back early. Okay?" Fran asked.

Phoebe bent down and cleaned off the bottom of her feet. "Make sure you clean your feet before you leave the kitchen," she told Fran. She glanced around the kitchen. "There isn't that much left to do. I think we've done a pretty good job so far. I'll see you later."

Fran straightened up and stretched. "God, my back is sore. I hope this is the last time I have to do this shit."

"It could be if you would just stop killing people," Phoebe replied sarcastically, as she walked out of the room.

CHAPTER SIXTEEN

Fran stared at the front door, waiting for Phoebe to open it and come in.

"Fran? Are you in there?" Phoebe called out, knocking on the door.

Fran got out of her chair, walked over to the door, and opened it. "It's about time you got home."

"I forgot my key."

"Did you have a good time?" Fran asked, looking at her watch. "Do you know what time it is?"

"Yes and yes. It was a lovely shower. Cassi looks like she could pop any time now. And, it's only a little after eleven."

"You said you'd come home early."

"Well, I didn't. Did you manage to finish up in the kitchen?"

"I guess. Why don't you go give it the white glove exam and tell me if you think it's good enough?"

"Why don't I go change my clothes instead? Or have you changed your mind about what to do with Gary?"

"No, I haven't changed my mind. But I'd rather get a few hours of sleep first. I'm exhausted."

Phoebe looked at her, wondering what Fran was planning now. "What time are you thinking of leaving?"

"In the morning."

"We can't leave when it's light outside. Fran. It's either tonight or we have to wait until tomorrow night."

"You're right. I'm not thinking straight. It's cold in the garage and he certainly isn't going to start to stink like Swinger did. What difference does it make if we do it tonight or tomorrow night? It gets dark early now. We could probably leave around five-thirty or six and be home by ten or so."

"What about his mom? Did you send her a text?"

"I did."

"You used his phone. Right?"

"Of course, I did. I told her that he missed her and was heading out to visit her for a few days," Fran replied.

"Did she text back?"

"She said she was looking forward to seeing him and she'd start making the spaghetti sauce. I texted back that his phone was dying and he'd let her know when he was leaving."

"Okay. That sounds good. I gather you plan on leaving his phone in his car."

"Well, dah. That way, if the cops check it, they'll see where he was and when."

"How do you feel, Fran? I know you liked him. A lot."

"I feel bad. It's going to take a while to get over this. We were good together, you know, but I would never have married him. Besides, after what he did to you, I doubt I would have ever trusted him again. I don't think you were the only one, either."

"What do you mean?"

"I went through the messages on his phone. There are quite a few texts from some women I never heard of.

97

They're kind of suggestive..." She turned away, trying to hold back the tears.

"I'm sorry."

"It's better that I found out now." Fran shrugged. "Men! Can't live with 'em and you can't live without them."

"You'll find someone else."

"I guess."

"So, you're, okay?"

Fran smiled. 'I'm okay. I'm just exhausted. And, I'm off to bed. I think we both need a good night's sleep."

"Night, Fran."

Fran walked into the kitchen and smiled. "Good morning."

"Hey, sleepyhead. Do you know what time it is?"

"I know it's after eleven. I slept like a log." She glanced toward the coffee pot. "That smells good."

"I'll pour you a cup," Phoebe said. "Do you want some toast or something?"

"Nah, just coffee for now."

Phoebe poured her a cup of coffee and handed it to her. "Sit a minute, will you? I think we need to talk."

Fran glanced at her, pulled out a chair, and sat down at the table. "What is it?"

"First of all, I want to say that you did an excellent job on this kitchen. I don't think it's ever been this clean."

Fran smiled. "Thanks."

"Fran, do you..." Phoebe took a deep breath.

"What?"

"This is hard. I was up most of the night, thinking about the two of us. I think we need help. I think we should see a therapist."

Fran stared at her for a moment, then laughed. "You're kidding. Right?"

"I'm serious, Fran. Think about what we've done in the past few days. The very fact that we are acting like this is all normal... Well, it's not. You killed a man you say you loved without blinking an eye. And, I don't see any real remorse from you at all. We should have called the police after you saved me from Swinger, but we didn't. The fact that we could cut him up and toss him out like garbage..."

"So, you're saying that you think we're both crazy, is that it?"

"I think we both have some serious issues. I did some research last night while you were sleeping. It's possible that you may have what is called a passive-aggressive personality. Maybe, I do, too. Now, that doesn't make us crazy, but it's a concern. However, there must be something lacking when two men are killed and we don't feel any regret or sorrow about it."

"You mean that I don't feel those things, don't you?"

"No, that's not what I said."

"I feel regret, Pheebs, and I'm sorry I killed Gary. I'm not sorry I killed that fat pig, though." Fran stood up and walked over to the sink, dumped out her cup, and set it in the sink. "Maybe you should have spent more time sleeping and less time screwing around on the computer last night. This is all a crock of bullshit."

"Is it? You said you were crazy in love with Gary and yet you killed him like he was nothing. I've never been in love. I turn off whenever a guy tries to get close. I think we both have problems."

"If you think you need help, by all means, go for it. I'm fine just the way I am. In fact, I like who I am. Anyway, crazy people don't know they are nuts. So, if you think we're crazy, we probably aren't. I think you should stop trying to play doctor."

"I'm not. However, I do think we both need to talk to somebody, Fran. If nothing else, we should try to figure out why we are at each other all the time."

"Good grief, Pheebs. We're sisters. Sisters fight. It doesn't mean we have a mental imbalance."

"Will you at least think about it?"

"I'm gonna go shower and get dressed. I have a few errands to run before we leave this afternoon."

"That's it? You're done talking?"

"About this nonsense? Yes," Fran told her. She turned and walked out of the room.

Phoebe shook her head, frustrated. "Shit."

"Son of a bitch," Fran yelled. "Try harder."

Phoebe let go of Gary and flinched as his feet hit the cement. "He's not going to bend. We're going to have to put him in the back seat."

"No!" Fran exclaimed. "I want him in the trunk."

"Fran, we can put him in the back seat and cover him with a blanket. Think about it. Later on, it will be a lot easier than trying to take him out of the trunk."

"I don't know."

"Please, Fran, let's just put him in the back seat."

Fran let go of her end of his body and Gary hit the floor headfirst. "I've got to rest a minute."

"Seriously? I mean, I know he's dead, but to just drop him like that is..."

"You're right. He's dead," Fran interrupted. "He didn't feel a thing," she added grinning.

Phoebe stared at her. "You think that was funny, don't you? See, this is the kind of crap I was talking about before."

"It was – kinda." Fran shrugged. "I can remember when you used to be fun."

"So, you think this is fun?"

"I guess not," Fran replied, smirking.

"I give up. Where did you put the gas can?" Phoebe asked.

"It's in the trunk of your car."

"Why my..." She thought for a moment. "That's good. In case I get stopped I can always say it's for my lawnmower."

"It's November. Are you still cutting grass in November?"

"It's for my snowblower. How's that?"

"Fine. And, please, don't get stopped by any cops."

"What about our phones? Should we take them? They could be traced later, you know."

"We'll take them but let's take the batteries out."

"Why not just leave them here? If something happens and one of us puts our battery back in, the other one won't know it. It doesn't make sense."

Fran glared at her. "So, now you're calling me stupid."

Phoebe took a deep breath and let it out. "No, I'm not. Can we just get on with this and stop the fighting, please?"

Fran shook her head yes. "Sorry. Let's see if we can get Gary in the back seat. Okay?"

"Okay," Phoebe said. She bent down and grabbed Gary's legs. "Ready? One, two, three, and lift."

"Ouch," Fran cried out.

"What's the matter?"

"I think I just pulled a muscle."

"How's your back?" Phoebe asked Fran as they walked into the kitchen.

"It's okay. I'll ice it tonight. It should feel fine tomorrow."

"I can't believe how well everything went," Phoebe declared.

"You said that already."

"I know. It's just that it went so smoothly. I can't believe it."

"Enough already," Fran said laughing. "What did you expect was going to happen?"

"I don't know. I'm just glad we're home safe and sound."

"That garbage bag in your trunk – that has Sammy in it, doesn't it?"

"Yeh. I'm sorry I was going to cut him up to look for that finger."

"How about we rebury him tomorrow? I'll collect all his things so we can bury those with him."

"We'll need a larger box. And, a bigger grave."

"I know. There are some boxes in the attic. I think there is one big enough for everything."

"Good. Why don't you get all that together while I make a cross?"

"How do you plan to do that?"

"We only need a couple of pieces of wood and some nails. There's some old wood in the garage. I'll nail two pieces together and paint his name on it. We can always pick up a nicer one later. Sound good?"

"Sounds good. Thank you, Pheebs."

"You're welcome. By the way, Sammy's been dead for a while now. I suggest you don't open the box that he's in. Just put that box in the bigger box."

"Got it."

"Well, I'm off to bed. See you in the morning."

"Thanks again, Pheebs."

CHAPTER SEVENTEEN

<u>Monday, November 8th</u>

"It seems strange to be going back to work," Fran commented. "I've gotten used to being at home."

"Did you miss it?"

"I guess a little. I like my job."

Phoebe looked Fran over and smiled. "You look great. I love that outfit on you."

"Thanks. What are you going to do today?"

"I think I might start baking Christmas cookies."

"Isn't it a little early?" Fran asked.

"Not really, considering only half of them make it into the freezer."

Fran laughed. "You do like your cookies."

"I do."

"You might want to check the want ads," Fran suggested.

"That's a given. I do that every day."

"Well, I'm off. I'll see you tonight."

"Fran?" Phoebe hesitated.

"What is it?"'

"How do you think I'd look as a blond?"

"Are you serious?" Fran asked her, laughing. "Why in the world would you change your hair color?"

"Being a brunette is boring and they say that blonds have more fun and stuff. Plus, I might have a little more luck getting a job if I was blond."

"And, it would also be an excuse for all the dumb things you do," Fran told her grinning.

"Yeah, well you're a Karen every now and then. What's your excuse?"

"We're all Karens now and then. Hey, if you want to go blond – go for it. You can always change it back if you don't like it. I really have to go. I'll see you tonight."

"See ya," Phoebe said. "I wish you didn't have to go. I've gotten used to you being around."

"Byeee," Fran exclaimed as she walked out of the door.

Phoebe decided to look around the kitchen, just to be sure that there was no blood splatter hiding that Fran may have missed. After about ten minutes, she poured herself a cup of coffee and sat down at the table. Suddenly, she jumped up and went to the sink, took the stopper out, and looked down the drain. "There just might be," she uttered.

She walked over to the utility room and took a bottle of ammonia off the shelf. She went back to the sink, closed the drain with the stopper, and poured half the bottle into the sink. "Whoa," she exclaimed, stepping away from the sink. She walked into the living room, took a deep breath, held it, ran to the sink, and yanked the stopper out of the drain hole. She dropped it into the sink and ran back to the living room.

That shit could kill a person, she thought. She waited a few minutes, went back to the sink, and turned on the water. *That should do it.* She thought about the sink and tub upstairs in the bathroom and wondered if those drains had been cleaned properly. She decided not to risk it. She would pour the rest of the ammonia down those drains. As she picked up the bottle, the doorbell rang. She looked toward the door, then looked at the bottle she was holding.

"I'll be right there," she yelled as she started toward the door, setting the bottle on a small table. "Oh, crap," she muttered, realizing that she was still in her nightgown. "Hold on," she shouted. She opened the door a few inches and looked to see who it was. "Yes?" she said softly.

"Good morning. I'm Detective Handy. I was by a few days ago and talked to Ms. Fran Figg. Do you…"

"I'm not dressed. Could you come back later?" Phoebe interrupted and started to close the door.

"Wait," Handy said loudly. "Are you Phoebe Figg?"

"Yes, but I can't talk now. I don't know anything anyway."

"How about you throw some clothes on? I'll wait for you out here."

"Well…" Phoebe looked behind her and then back at the detective.

"I only need to ask you a few questions," Handy said. "It will only take a few minutes."

Phoebe sighed. "All right. Wait here."

Thirteen minutes later, wearing an old pair of jeans and a sweatshirt, Phoebe opened the door. "You can come in now."

Detective Handy looked her up and down. "It took you that long to put that on?"

"I can change into something else if this isn't good enough for you," she retorted.

"No, I'm sorry. I didn't mean anything by that." He sniffed the air.

"What are you doing?" Phoebe asked. "Does something smell?"

"I wanted to see if your house smelled the same as it did the last time I was here."

"Does it?"

"No. Now, I think I smell ammonia."

"You do. I just cleaned the kitchen."

"You ladies sure keep a clean house. I wish my wife would take a few lessons from you."

"We don't give lessons. Did somebody tell you that we give lessons?"

"No, it was just... I meant." He looked at the couch. "Never mind. Do you mind if we sit?"

"Of course. How about the kitchen? Would you like a cup of coffee?"

"Thanks."

"How do you take it?"

"Black. Thanks."

"This way." Phoebe turned and walked into the kitchen. Assuming that the detective was following her, she walked to the counter, picked up the coffee pot, and turned. "You said black..." He wasn't there. "Detective?"

"That smell is a little too strong for me," he answered from the doorway. "Do you mind if we sit in here?"

Phoebe shrugged. "That's fine. Do you still want coffee?"

"Thanks, but I think I'll pass."

Phoebe rolled her eyes and walked into the living room. "Please, sit down."

Handy took a small black notebook and pen out of his jacket pocket and sat down on the couch. He flipped through the pages until he found the one he was looking for."

"So?" Phoebe prompted.

"I assume you know that Pastor Swinger went missing a few days ago."

"Yes, I heard. It was on Halloween, wasn't it?"

"Right."

"I hate Halloween. It seems bad things always happen on Halloween, doesn't it?"

"Did something bad happen to you on Halloween?"

"No. I mean, like Pastor Swinger disappearing. That's bad news, isn't it?" Phoebe replied.

"Of course," Handy agreed. "Can you tell me when you last saw him?" he asked, starting to write in his notebook.

"I saw him that day."

Handy's head jerked up and he stared at Phoebe. "You saw him the day he disappeared?

"That's right. He stopped by for a few minutes that afternoon. He wanted to see how we were doing."

"You mean you and your sister, Fran?"

"Right."

"I recall your sister saying that she hadn't seen him since your mom's funeral. My condolences, by the way."

"Thank you. She probably hadn't. She was out when he came over and I don't recall her telling me that she had talked to him on any other occasion."

"How long was he here?"

"Not long. Maybe ten or fifteen minutes," Phoebe grinned. "Long enough to eat half a batch of my cookies."

"I understand he did like his sweets," Handy declared, smiling.

"If you could eat it, he liked it. He had a huge appetite. You know, when food was served at church functions, you wanted to be sure you were in front of him in the line or you'd go hungry," Phoebe told him, grinning.

"Can you tell me what time of the day he was here?"

Phoebe thought for a moment. "I'm not one hundred percent sure, but I think it was around one-thirty or so. I know he was gone by two, for sure."

"And, you haven't seen him since?"

"Nope. Do you have any idea where he is?"

"We're working on a few ideas. Did he mention anything to you?"

"No. I mean, like if I knew I would have told you before now. He wasn't here that long."

"Do you have a job, Ms. Figg?"

"Please call me Phoebe. No. I'm between jobs right now. It's hard to find work these days."

"I'm sure you'll find something soon." Handy stood up and walked to the door. "Thank you for your time. If you think of anything, please give me a call." He handed her his business card. "This is my number."

Phoebe took the card and looked at it. "Thanks, I will." She hesitated a moment. "Well, there is one thing."

"What would that be?"

"How do you think I'd look as a blond? I'm thinking of dying my hair."

Handy stared at her for a moment and shook his head up and down. "I think being a blond would fit you just fine."

CHAPTER EIGHTEEN

Phoebe sat back from her computer. "Wow!" she mumbled, with a surprised look on her face. "I didn't think that would happen so fast." She responded to the message on Facebook Marketplace and waited. The reply was quick. The sender wanted to pick up the living room set this afternoon. She thought for a moment. "Why not?" she decided, typed in her response, and hit send. Arrangements were made within the next few messages for pickup and it was agreed that Mike Myers would be there at one o'clock.

Phoebe walked out of the room, grinning. One of two things was going to happen. Fran was either going to be glad to see that the old couch and chair were gone or she would go ballistic. Either way, they were going to have to go shopping for a new living room set.

She picked up her phone and called Fran, who answered on the third ring. "I wondered how long it would be before you called. What's up?" Fran asked.

"Are you busy?" Phoebe asked.

"Of course, I'm busy. What is it, Pheebs?"

"Are you coming right home after work tonight?"

"I plan on it. Why?"

"Just wondered."

"Are you fixing dinner?"

"I guess I can. I haven't got much else to do. Is there anything special you want? You know, to celebrate your first day back at work."

"Not really. You pick something. How's the job hunting going?"

"Same as usual. Nothing to get excited about."

"Don't get discouraged. I'm sure something will turn up soon."

"I know. And, Fran?"

"Yes."

"I have a surprise for you," Phoebe told her.

Fran had a sinking feeling in her stomach. "Pheebs? What did you do?" she asked quietly.

"Well, if I told you, you wouldn't be surprised. See you later," Phoebe said and ended the call.

Mike Myers was one minute early to pick up the living room furniture. He rang the bell and waited.

Phoebe swung open the door and smiled. "Mike?"

"That's me," Myers replied. "This is George," he told her, nodding at the man standing next to him.

"It's nice to meet you both. Man, you're right on time."

"Time is valuable and I never like to keep a lady waiting."

"Come on in and take a look." Phoebe glanced over Mike's shoulder. "I see you brought a truck."

"Always need to be prepared," Mike replied.

"This is it," Phoebe told him, pointing to the couch and chair.

"Ah-huh." Mike walked over to it and checked it out. "What do you think, George?" he asked his friend.

"Looks good to me. If you don't buy it, I will."

"I'll take it. What was the agreed price again?"

Phoebe grinned. "I think you remember that it was six hundred dollars."

"Will you take five?"

Phoebe pursed her lips, thinking about his offer. "Well, we agreed on six, but I..."

"I'll give you six," George interrupted.

Mike turned and glared at him. "Great friend you are."

"Five-fifty and it's yours," Phoebe told Mike.

"Done." He counted out the money and handed it to Phoebe. "Come on, George. Let's load them up."

Phoebe paced back and forth in the kitchen, getting more nervous by the minute. Fran had just pulled her car into the garage and Phoebe was second-guessing her decision to sell the furniture. She already figured that Fran was going to go crazy.

"Hi. Something smells good," Fran said as she walked into the kitchen.

"Hi," Phoebe said, still pacing. "Good day back at work?"

"It was good. I'm glad to be back." Fran observed her pacing for a moment and started to get worried. "What did you do, Pheebs?"

Phoebe stopped pacing and looked at her sister. "What makes you think I did anything?"

"You only pace when you're upset about something."

I think I might have done a dumb thing."

"So, what else is new?"

"I'm serious, Fran."

"Sorry. What dumb thing?"

"Go look in the living room."

Fran walked over to the door that led into the living room and stared. She turned and looked at Phoebe. "Would you like to tell me where our furniture is?" she asked, her voice slightly more than a whisper.

"I sold it."

"I see. Why did you do that?"

"Please don't get mad," Phoebe begged, as she started to cry. "I know I shouldn't have."

"Damned right you shouldn't have. Who did you sell it to?"

"I man named Mike. He bought it on Facebook."

"You listed our furniture for sale on Facebook?"

"They have this place called Market Place where you can buy and sell stuff and I thought we should get some new furniture, so I listed it just to see if anyone was interested and the Mike guy bought it and I'm so sorry."

"Take a breath, Pheebs."

"I don't think it was even on there for more than thirty minutes before it sold," she added.

"I know what Market Place is." Fran sat down at the kitchen table and glared at her sister. "Did it ever occur to you to ask me what I thought about selling our couch and chair? You know, before you did this?"

"I was going to, but then I got so excited when it sold..."

"That's not what I asked you. Why didn't you discuss this with me before – notice I said before – you decided to sell it?"

"I don't know. I guess I wanted to surprise you. I got five hundred and fifty dollars for it."

Fran looked surprised. "For that old crap? Well, at least you didn't give it away."

"So, do you want to go shopping after we eat?" Phoebe asked.

Fran shook her head. "I swear, Pheebs, you will..."

"I know. I'm gonna be the death of you. Well, do you?"

"What I'd like is for you to call that Mike guy and tell him you've changed your mind and you want our furniture back."

"He won't give it back."

"You called him already?"

"I felt bad after he left – you know, like buyer's remorse only this was seller's regret. Anyway, I called him and he said he wouldn't give it back. He said his wife loved it and he was going to keep it. I even offered to give him an extra fifty dollars. No 'takebacks', he said. Can you believe that? Like we were kids or something."

Fran sighed. "It doesn't look like we've got much choice, does it? I guess we'll have to go furniture shopping."

"Thank you, Fran. I know you're going to love getting new furniture. Everything we have is so outdated. We need to spruce up this place a little."

Fran looked at Phoebe. "I thought you were going to color your hair. Did you change your mind?"

"Oh, I'm going blond all right. Even Detective Handy thinks I'd look good as a blond. I made an appointment with Sylvia for Thursday."

"Did I hear you right? Why would Detective Handy think that?" Fran asked looking confused.

"Oh, yeah," Phoebe replied nervously. "There's something else I need to tell you."

"I need a drink. Is there any Jack Daniels in the cupboard or did we drink it all?"

"I'll fix it for you."

Fran kicked off her heels and sat back in the chair.

"Water or soda?" Phoebe asked her.

"Water on the side, please. When did you talk to Detective Handy?"

"He stopped by and asked a few questions about Pastor Swinger. He said they don't have a clue where he is."

"I already talked to him. Did he say why he came back?"

"He was just covering all his bases, I guess. He wanted to talk to me, too."

"That's it?"

"That's all." Phoebe handed Fran her drink. "Here's to life getting back to normal," she said as she clinked her glass on Fran's."

"Thanks," Fran said, yawning. "God, I'm tired. It's gonna take a few days to get back into the swing of things."

"Fran, do you remember the last time Gary was here and ..."

"Of course, I remember when he was here. Why are you bringing that up?" Fran interrupted.

"I wonder why no one has come looking for him," Phoebe commented. "Don't you think his mother would have informed somebody by now? You know, that he didn't show up."

"You would think so, wouldn't you?" Fran agreed, grinning mischievously.

Phoebe stared at her for a moment. "You look like the cat that swallowed the canary. You did something, didn't you?"

"I sent her a text telling her that Gary had a situation and couldn't make it."

Phoebe took a sip of her drink, taking in what Fran had just told her. "I don't get it."

"Gary had a highly secretive job. I promised him that I would never talk about what he did. I think the only two outsiders who knew what he did were his mother and me.

"So, what was it?"

"Gary did special work for the government and sometimes his assignments would last for months. The good news is if Gary doesn't show up for six months or even longer, no one is going to report him missing. It wouldn't be unusual."

"What kind of assignments."

"I'm not exactly sure, but I do know that they were dangerous. Sometimes he went into enemy areas in different countries to obtain information. He never said for sure, but I'm pretty sure he worked for the CIA."

"Noo!" Phoebe declared, shocked by what Fran had told her. "He was one of those black op guys, wasn't he? They don't even acknowledge their own people if they get into trouble."

"You can never tell anyone, Pheebs. Promise?"

"Of course, I promise. Besides, who would I tell? What did you tell Gary's mom when you texted her?"

"Just what I said. That he was contacted on his way to Dubuque and had to detour back to Chicago. I said he was upset about not seeing her and that he would most likely be gone over the holidays."

"Didn't she question why you sent the text and not him? That seems strange."

"It does, but I think she was used to strange when it came to him."

"Did he ever kill anyone?" Phoebe asked.

"He never said for sure but I think he probably did. Anyway, let's just forget about him, shall we?"

"Sure. What I was going to ask you before we started discussing Gary was..." She looked away. "That day in the living room when we saw the finger in the couch. Do you remember?"

"Of course. You tried to get the finger out of the couch while I distracted Gary and..." She stopped, took a big swallow of her drink, and set the glass down. She gave Phoebe an inquiring look. "What about it?"

"And, the second time I tried to pull the finger out, it broke off. Remember?"

"Yes," Fran replied hesitantly.

"Then, we got all busy cleaning the spilled milk off Gary's trousers and everything and I told you that you couldn't see the finger anymore and..." Phoebe took a deep breath and let it out. "Well, I was wondering if later on... Well, did you remove the rest of the finger? You know, from between the cushions?"

Fran thought for a second about what Phoebe had just asked her. "You fucking idiot," Fran yelled, as it sunk in. She picked up her glass and threw it at her sister, hitting her on the right temple.

Phoebe's head jerked back and she slowly slid out of her chair onto the floor.

Fran looked at the empty chair. "You better be dead, Pheebs, because if you're not, I swear I'm gonna kill you." She went over to a kitchen cabinet, took out a clean glass, and emptied the remaining whiskey into it. She took a sip, turned, and looked at Phoebe who was out cold on the floor. "Ah, crap. It looks like it's gonna be a long night," she mumbled.

CHAPTER NINETEEN

Phoebe opened her eyes, saw Fran standing over her, and shrieked. "Stay away from me," she ordered. She grabbed a chair to steady herself and she pushed herself up off the floor."

"I'm sorry," Fran said. "I didn't mean to hurt you." She reached out to help Phoebe, who moved further away. "Don't you fucking touch me."

"I said I was sorry."

"You need help, Fran. You have some serious anger issues. One of these days, you're gonna kill someone. Oh, wait. Whoops. You already did."

"Only because I was trying to save you from getting raped."

"Really? Tell me, what was Gary doing that was so horrible that you had to kill him? I sell some old furniture and that's a good enough excuse to try to kill me?

"I wasn't trying to kill you but if I had you would have deserved it. How could you leave that finger in the couch?"

"Me? You're just as much to blame as I am. All the burners on your stove aren't working, Fran. You need some repair work done on your brain."

"I told you before that there's nothing wrong with me. So, what if I've got a little temper? Doesn't everyone?

You sound just like mom, going on and on about me needing help."

Phoebe looked surprised. "What do you mean? I never heard mom say anything about your anger issues."

"Well, she did. She was constantly at me to get help. It's a good thing she died when she did or..."

"Or, what?" Phoebe asked her.

"Nothing,"

"You would have killed her. Is that what you were going to say?"

"Of course not. Don't be an ass." Fran took a sip of her drink and put the glass down on the table. "Can I fix you one? Whoops. Sorry, I drank it all. It's all gone."

Phoebe turned and walked out of the kitchen. "I'm going to go lay down," she called out. "You better turn off the oven before the house burns down."

"Yes, Mother," Fran yelled back.

Friday, November 12th

"It's gorgeous," Fran declared. "The color is absolutely perfect. What time was it delivered?"

Phoebe continued reading her magazine, ignoring her.

"Pheebs?"

Phoebe turned a page and continued to read.

"Are you ever going to talk to me? I said I was sorry a million times. What else can I do?"

Phoebe turned another page.

"Is the chair comfortable? I thought it was in the store, but you just never know until you get it home." She gazed at her sister. "Please, please, Pheebs. It's been days since you said a word and it's driving me nuts. Talk to me."

Phoebe put the magazine down and looked over at Fran. "You want me to talk? Will you even listen to what I have to say?"

"Of course, I will. I can't stand it when you're mad at me. Please, tell me what I can do to make it up to you."

"Sit down, Fran." Phoebe waited until her sister was settled on the couch facing her.

"Tell me," Fran prompted.

"I want to sell the house. I don't want to live here anymore."

"You're crazy," Fran exclaimed, angrily. "I'm not selling my house."

"See, this is exactly what I'm talking about. You fly right off the handle before you even hear what I have to say. And, it's our house, not your house."

"It's more mine than yours."

"How do you figure that?"

"I've lived here longer than you have."

"Only because you were born first. Please, will you be quiet for a moment and let me finish?"

"All right. So, finish already."

"Mom left the house to both of us. One of these days one of us will find someone and move out. At least I hope so. This house is way too big for the two of us. It takes a lot to keep it going. I want my money. If you don't want to sell, then consider buying me out. I'm sure a bank will give you a loan, considering what this house is worth. You'd have more than enough equity with your half. And, that's all the collateral they should need."

Fran stared at her. "When did you become a loan officer?" she asked sarcastically.

"I've done my homework, Fran. This house is easily worth around five hundred thousand. Think about it. Wouldn't you rather have half of the money and start fresh someplace else? With that and the cash that mom left us, we would have enough to do almost anything we want."

"What are you going to do when your money runs out?"

"I plan on getting a job."

Fran smirked. "That's a good one. Doing what? You're not qualified to do anything except eat cookies."

"I've talked to an attorney, Fran," Phoebe said, ignoring the dig. "He said I can force a sale. However, I'd rather not do that."

"I'm not moving," Fran declared, struggling to hold her temper. "I was born here and I'll die here. If you want to move out – well, be my guest. We should have parted ways a long time ago."

"Is that your final answer? You want to stay here?"

"It is."

"Fine. Then, I expect you to make arrangements to buy me out. I'd like to be out of here by the first of the year."

Fran's lower lip started to quiver, as she fought back her tears. "How could you do this to me," she whined. "After all I've done for you, this is the way you treat me?"

"It's time, Fran. Gary was right when he said you treat me like you're my mother. I'm twenty-five years old. I need to be on my own. That will never happen if I continue to live here."

"I never should have killed Gary," Fran acknowledged quietly. "That's why you want to leave, isn't it?"

"Maybe, a little bit. Mostly because I'm tired of the fighting."

"What are you talking about? We get along great," Fran interjected, looking genuinely surprised at Phoebe's comment.

"No, Fran, we don't. Sometimes we do, but mostly we fight. I'm tired of it. I'm tired of never knowing what kind of a storm you're bringing into the house when you walk through the door. There are sunshiny days, I'll admit, but most of the time there's a tornado coming through that door when you walk in."

"So, it's all me, is it?"

"Of course not. It's both of us."

Fran sighed and stood up. "I'm sorry you feel this way. I really am. If you want to leave, I'm not going to try to stop you. I'll make arrangements tomorrow to talk to the bank about a mortgage."

"Thank you. I truly believe that it's for the best."

Fran turned and walked toward the kitchen. "Of course," she uttered, "if you weren't around, everything would be all mine."

"Don't even think about it, Fran."

"Just talking out loud, Sister."

"You can talk all you want, but I've made arrangements to make sure you'll spend the rest of your life in prison if anything happens to me."

Fran looked back at Phoebe. "My, my, my. Weren't you a busy little girl today?"

CHAPTER TWENTY

"Tomorrow is Thanksgiving," Fran mentioned.

Phoebe looked up from her book. "I'm aware," she replied.

"Are you fixing a turkey?"

"Not this year, Fran. I'm spending Thanksgiving with some friends."

Fran looked surprised. "What friends?"

"What are you doing tomorrow?" Phoebe asked, ignoring Fran's question.

"I thought I'd be spending the day with you," Fran told her, showing her disappointment. "We always spend the holidays together."

"I'm sorry, but things have changed."

"What do you expect me to do?" Fran whined.

"That's up to you. Don't you have some friends you can spend it with? Or, maybe you could drive over to Aunt Betty's and have dinner with her family. She always puts on a great spread. Why don't you give her a call?" Phoebe turned the page in her book and continued reading.

Fran glared at her. "God, you are such a bitch," she said, raising her voice.

"Fran, I'm sorry you feel that way. But you have to get it through your head that we aren't joined at the hip.

I'm making a life for myself now and you need to do the same."

"I see. And, does that mean that we are done doing things together? No more spending holidays together or going out to dinner or anything?"

"Of course not. After all, we are sisters. It's just that we won't spend as much time together as before. We'll still see each other."

"I don't like this one bit. Too many things are changing."

"You'll adjust. By the way, did you get your loan approval?"

"I'll know next week. Don't worry. I'm sure it will go through and you'll get your money."

"I'm not worried. Just curious, that's all."

Fran stared at her. "You're sure you want to do this moving out thing?" she asked after a few moments.

Phoebe smiled. "Yes, I'm sure, and will you quit staring at me."

"I thought you were going to go blond."

"I changed my mind."

"You've changed, Pheebs. You aren't the same person you were a few weeks ago."

"I hope it's for the better."

"I don't like the new you. You're no fun anymore."

"I'm sorry you feel that way."

Fran sat back on the couch and sighed. "Seriously, I don't even know who you are."

"Oh," Phoebe exclaimed. "Did I mention that I got a job? I start on Monday."

"Really?" Fran declared. "Where at? Testing cookies at a cookie factory?"

Phoebe shook her head, offended by Fran's comment. "Forget it," she said sadly. "I'm sorry I mentioned it."

"So, where is it?"

"Never mind." Phoebe stood up and stretched. "I need to take a walk. Would you like to join me?"

"It's cold out," Fran replied.

"It's fifty-seven degrees outside."

Fran shook her head no. "Maybe later."

"Don't say I didn't ask," Phoebe told her, smiling. "I'll see you later."

"Whatever," Fran replied, looking away.

"Come on, Fran, don't be like that. Come with me. A walk in the nice fresh air will be good for both of us. Let's walk down to Teddy's and get a cup of hot chocolate."

"We've got hot chocolate here. Besides, Teddy's is a long walk. I'm not up to it." Fran watched her sister put on her coat and gloves and leave the house. She wiped away a single tear as it rolled down her cheek.

What made her so different? she wondered. *I used to be the strong one, the one in charge, and now it's like that person never existed. Somehow our roles have been reversed and I don't like it one bit. Not one little bit. I think Miss High and Mighty needs to be taken down a peg or two.*

"Or, three," she said grinning. "One for the money, two for the show, three to get ready," she said in a sing-song voice, reciting the old nursery rhyme. "Time to get ready, Fran. Time to take back the power." She laughed as she skipped into the kitchen, yelling, "and, four to go!"

"Aunt Betty, this is Fran. I was wondering what you have going on tomorrow."

"Fran, it's nice to hear from you. How are you and Phoebe doing?"

"We're fine. The reason I'm calling is that I don't have any plans for tomorrow. Do you think you have room for one more person?"

"Oh, dear. I'm not sure, Fran. Hold on a moment?"

Fran tapped her nails against her phone, waiting for her aunt to get back to her.

"What about Phoebe? Does she want to come, too?

"Phoebe? Oh, no, she's spending the day with some friends. Listen, if you don't have room, that's fine. Don't worry about it."

"Well, we can't have you spending the day alone, can we? Dinner is around five."

"Oh, thank you so much. I was dreading spending the day alone. Can I bring anything?"

"We're fine. The menu is set. Besides, when did you learn how to cook? I thought Phoebe was the cook."

"She is, but I do have a few special dishes I make," Fran told her as she looked out the living room window.

"You can tell me all about them tomorrow, dear."

"Thanks, Aunt Betty. Bye."

Fran hung up the phone and sighed. Her aunt tended to talk non-stop and repeat things over and over, but it was still better than giving Phoebe the satisfaction of thinking she was spending the day all alone.

Betty hung up the phone and looked at her husband. "Fran is coming to dinner tomorrow," she told him.

"Are you serious? Why did you invite her? She's a pain in the ass, Betty. She'll ruin the whole day."

"She's my sister's daughter. I couldn't tell her she couldn't come."

"Well, she better leave her crazy at home, 'cause I'm not putting up with it."

"Please, don't get upset. It's only for a few hours."

"Is Phoebe coming, too?" he asked Betty.

"No, just Fran."

"It would be better if Phoebe was coming. She's the funny one."

CHAPTER TWENTY-ONE

Tuesday, November 30th

"I'm off," Fran yelled as she buttoned her coat.

"Wait a minute," Phoebe called to her.

"What is it? I'm running late."

"It's been three weeks, Fran. I'm beginning to worry about this so-called loan you said you're getting. I've had to put a hold on the place I moving to and I'm getting a little pressure from the owners. What's the story?"

"I'm not sure what the hang-up is. I'll give the bank a call over my lunch hour. Sorry, but I've got to go." Fran opened the door and ran out to the garage.

Phoebe bit her lip, trying not to say something she'd regret later. She was getting more and more concerned that Fran was stringing her along. *I can't trust her. Perhaps I should call the bank and find out what is going on*, she thought.

She glanced around the kitchen and made a face. Fran hadn't cleaned up from her dinner last night and dirty dishes were all over the counter and in the sink. Phoebe decided to give the house a once-over before she went out. It was her day off and she had shopping to do. As she started clearing the dishes and putting them into the dishwasher, she made a mental note to call the bank as soon as it opened.

Phoebe was so angry she was shaking. "I fucking knew she would pull something like this," she blurted out."

She sat back in her chair and thought about what she should do. *I guess I better call and cancel the apartment. Obviously, I won't have the money in time. Oh, shit. I almost forgot about the furniture. I'll have to cancel that or at least see what options I have. I swear to God if she was here right now, I'd...* Hearing the doorbell ring, Phoebe looked over at the front door wondering who it could be. She walked over to the front door and opened it. "Detective Handy," she stated, surprised to see him.

"Ms. Figg." He acknowledged.

She stared at him, waiting for him to continue. "Yes? Can I help you with something?" she finally asked when he just stared at her.

"You didn't go blond," he said, smiling.

"No, I changed my mind."

"I'm glad. You look good as a brunette."

"Thank you." She continued to hold the door open, wondering why he was here.

"May I come in?"

"What is it now? Do you have news of Pastor Swinger?"

"I have a couple of questions I'd like you to clear up if you don't mind. Is your sister here?"

"She's at work." She opened the door wider, stepped aside, and motioned for him to come in. "Please, have a seat."

Handy glanced over at the new furniture and smiled. "Nice. Very nice. You have good taste."

"My sister picked it out."

"Then, I guess she has good taste."

Phoebe sat down across from him and waited.

"Do you know Mrs. Grassler?"

"Of course. I've known her for years. She lives across the street." She gave him a questioning look. 'What about her?"

"We took a statement from her after Pastor Swinger went missing. At that time, she told us that she hadn't seen him on that day. The second time we interviewed her, she said she remembers seeing him go into your house around one-thirty. That time agrees with what you previously told me."

"That's right."

"You mentioned that Pastor Swinger was here for around fifteen minutes and that he was gone by two. Is that correct?"

Phoebe thought for a moment. "Yes, that's right."

"Well, Ms. Figg…

"Please, call me Phoebe."

"Well, Phoebe, Mrs. Grassler has recently come forward and said that she never saw the pastor leave your house."

"I'm sorry, but that's not right. Of course, he left. Besides, how would she know if he left or not?"

"Well, it seems she likes to watch her neighbors. She said that she sat and watched your house until almost three-thirty and that he was still here. In fact, the lady has quite an imaginative mind. She suggested that perhaps there was some hanky panky going on."

Phoebe sat back and grinned. "Detective Handy, have you ever seen Pastor Swinger?"

"Not in person, but I've seen pictures of him."

Phoebe stared at him.

"Oh, of course. You and him..." Handy smiled. "I don't see it happening."

"Thank you. It didn't. As I said, he left before two, Detective. I don't know what else I can tell you."

"It just seems strange that his car was still there the next day."

"I agree. However, Pastor Swinger has quite a few congregants on this street and he could have gone and visited any one of them after he left here."

"I guess that's a possibility," Handy said.

"Detective, did Mrs. Grassler also mention that she has a very weak bladder? It may sound mean, but she's been the butt of quite a few jokes regarding her condition. I don't think she can go for more than a half-hour before she needs to use the washroom. There is no way she could have looked out of her window for that long without taking a potty break."

Handy grinned. "She forgot to mention that part."

"I don't know why she would tell you that he never left. My mother and she were extremely close friends and I can't imagine why she would..." Phoebe shrugged. "I'm not even going to try to second guess why people do what they do."

Handy looked at her, reached up, scratched his cheek, and looked puzzled.

"Is there something else?"

"You're different."

"Excuse me?"

"I'm sorry, but you seem different to me."

"Thank you. I decided it was time to grow up. I have a job now and I'm getting ready to move into my own place soon. I guess I got tired of my sister taking care of me."

"Good for you. I like the new you."

"Why, Detective Handy, are you flirting a little?"

Handy grinned. "Nah, my wife wouldn't like it." He stood up and walked over to the door. "Thanks for your help, Phoebe. Hopefully, I won't have to bother you again."

"You can bother me any time you want," Phoebe replied.

"Now who is doing the flirting?" Handy laughed.

"See ya, Detective," she said, smiling as she closed the door behind him.

"I fixed dinner," Phoebe told Fran.

"Oh, no. That's so nice of you, Pheebs, but I'm going out for dinner. Sorry, it looks like you'll have to eat alone."

"No problem," Phoebe said, as she wiped off the counter. "Guess who came visiting today?"

Fran shrugged. "I haven't a clue."

"Our friendly cop, Detective Handy."

"What did he want?" Fran asked, looking concerned.

"He had a few more questions. It seems that Mrs. Grassler told him Swinger never left our house."

"Why the hell would she tell him that?"

"I have no idea, but I think I convinced him that she was wrong."

"You better have convinced him. I don't want him hanging around here asking a lot of questions. You're bound to mess up eventually."

"Thanks for your confidence in me, Fran."

"For crying out loud, Pheebs, do you have to take everything so personal?"

"Does that mean I shouldn't take it personally that you haven't applied for a mortgage on the house?"

Fran's head jerked up and she stared at Phoebe. "I don't know what you're talking about. Of course, I have."

"Not according to our bank, you haven't."

"I didn't go to our bank, you twit. I used a different bank. And, for your information, the loan has been approved and we close next Friday."

Phoebe looked surprised. "Really? I'm sorry, Fran. I guess it was taking so long that I got suspicious. Seriously, this is great news. Will you excuse me? I got some phone calls to make."

Fran watched Phoebe walk into the living room, seething that her sister would check up on her. *This shit has to end*, Fran thought. *I am so done with her.*

CHAPTER TWENTY-TWO

<u>Monday, December 6th</u>

"All right! Hold your horses. I'm coming," Fran shouted as she ran down the stairs. She stopped by the front door, hesitant to open it. "Who is it?" she yelled.

"Ms. Figg, I'm Detective Thompson and this is Sergeant Callahan from the police. Please open up."

Fran's heart started to pound. What in the world would the police want at one o'clock in the morning?

"I'm opening the door a little bit. Please show me your identification." She waited until Thompson showed her his badge through the small opening.

"We're legit, ma'am. Please open the door."

Fran opened the door, concern written on her face. "What is it?"

"May we come in for a moment?"

"Of course." Fran led the two officers to the couch. "Please, sit down."

"We're very sorry to inform you that your sister, Phoebe, was killed in a car accident this evening. We are very sorry for your loss."

Fran stared at them. "That can't be right. You must have her mistaken for someone else."

"I'm sorry, but there is no doubt it is her."

"Noo!" Fran cried out. "No, no, no. It can't be her," she moaned, crying hysterically. "It can't be. Not Phoebe. Please, dear God, not my Phoebe."

"We're so sorry. Is there someone you would like us to call?" Thompson asked her.

Fran glanced up at him and shook her head no. "There's no one," she sobbed.

"Go get her a glass of water," Thompson told Callahan.

Fran continued sobbing while Thompson sat and stared at her. "Is there anything I can do?" he finally asked her, looking uncomfortable.

She shook her head no and reached for a tissue. "I'm sorry," she told him as she wiped her eyes. "This is such a shock." She took the glass of water from Callahan and took a long swallow. "Thank you," she said. "Can you tell me what happened?"

"As you probably know, we had our first snowfall tonight. It melted right away making the streets wet. It seems that your sister drove up to a red light and when she tried to stop... Well, she either slid into the intersection or her brakes failed. I'm leaning toward the brakes failing, as it wasn't that slippery. There was a semi and..." The officer looked away. "I'm sorry, but he hit her on the driver's side of her car. It looks like he might have been going too fast for the conditions. Emergency was on the scene within minutes, but it was too late. She was killed immediately."

Fran put her face in her hands and sobbed. "My poor Pheebs," she wailed. "What am I to do now?"

"Rest assured, there will be a thorough and complete investigation into what happened. The driver of the truck has been ticketed for driving too fast for the conditions. Our forensic department will examine what is left of her car and try to determine if it was her brakes or the weather conditions..."

"Her brakes?" Fran interrupted. "Well, I can guarantee you it wasn't her brakes," Fran said, indignantly. "She took excellent care of her car."

"Of course. I'm sure she did," Detective Thompson agreed. He looked over at Callahan. "Let's go."

"Wait," Fran said.

"Yes?"

"What did you mean when you said what is left of her car? Just how bad is it?"

"Unfortunately, the impact caused the fuel tank to explode. The fire was pretty severe," Thompson told her, looking uncomfortable.

"And, Phoebe?"

"I'm sorry, but she didn't make it out of the car."

Fran looked up at them, tears running down her cheeks. "Thank you for letting me know. What do I do now?"

"Someone will contact you tomorrow – this afternoon and let you know."

"I see." Fran stood up and walked the officers to the door. "I'll want to see her."

"I don't think that's a good idea, Ms. Figg. There isn't enough..."

"I get it. You don't have to say anything else. Thank you again," she said as she closed the door.

She closed her eyes, took a deep breath, and let it out. "Assholes."

CHAPTER TWENTY-THREE

Tuesday, December 14th

Janice Myers dropped the towel she was using to dry the dishes and ran into the living room. Her two-year-old son, Perry, was screaming as blood poured out of his cheek.

"Mike!" Janice screamed. "Get in here and bring a towel. Perry's bleeding." She looked over at Jon, who was on the floor looking scared and crying. "What happened?" she asked him, as she picked Perry up and ran to the kitchen. "Mike, where are you?"

"I didn't do it," Jon yelled after her. "He got hurt by the couch."

Mike opened the bathroom door, pulled his zipper up, and ran into the kitchen. "What the hell happened? What's going on?"

"Here, take him." She handed Mike their son, reached for a towel, put it on the little boy's face, and held it tight. "Hold onto that," she instructed her husband. "I'm going to get a cloth to wipe off the blood and try to see what we're dealing with."

"What the hell happened?" Mike asked again.

"Jon says the couch hurt him, whatever that means." She held up a wet, warm cloth, pulled the towel

138

away, and started to wash off the wound. "It's okay, baby," she said soothingly to her screaming child. She looked at Mike. "It's a pretty deep puncture, Mike. We need to get him to the emergency room."

"Get the kids' coats," he said, still holding the screaming child.

"Jon, get your coat on. We need to take Perry to the hospital to get him fixed." She grabbed the boys' coats from off the hooks, tossed Jon his, and ran into the kitchen.

"Let's go," Mike yelled. "And bring a few more towels. He's bleeding like a stuck pig."

"I'm gonna fucking kill that bitch," Mike whispered as they put the sleeping boys down on their beds. He pulled a blanket over Perry and tucked it under his chin. "Poor little guy," he said softly.

"I doubt she knew it was there, Mike. She certainly would have removed it if she had known," Janice replied, as they walked out of the boys' bedroom. "Anyway, I've told the boys a million times not to jump on the furniture."

"You're blaming the boys for this?" Mike yelled.

"Shh. You'll wake the kids. Of course not. I'm not sure who's to blame. I cleaned that couch the day you brought it home. I sure didn't see that thing in it."

"Well, I sure as hell didn't put it there. As far as I know, we have all of our fingers. It had to be there when we bought it."

"God, Mike, do you know how lucky we are that he didn't put an eye out with that thing?"

"Believe me, I've thought about it. I'm calling the police."

"What do you expect them to do?"

"Well, for one, I think they might want to find out where the finger came from. Or, do you think it's every day that fingers pop up out of couches and no one cares where they came from? Think for a moment, Janice."

She slapped herself gently on her forehead and grinned. "Sorry. It's been a long day."

Mike unfolded a napkin and laid the finger on it. He carefully wrapped it up and put it on the top shelf of a bookcase.

"Why up there?" Janice asked.

"So, Jon can't get at it," he told her. "I know if I was four years old, my curiosity would get the better of me."

"Want a beer?" Janice asked him.

"So much."

She smiled. "I think I'll join you."

Detective Handy looked up from his desk and watched as his boss, Captain Trumble, who was unusually animated, hung up his phone. "What was that all about?" Handy called to him from across the room.

Trumble shook his head. "Some damn fool says he found a finger in his couch. Says his kid almost poked his eye out. He wants us to go pick it up."

Handy felt a familiar sensation travel through his body. His gut instinct was kicking in and his mind jumped immediately to the Figg sisters. "Did he say what color the couch was?" Handy asked.

"What the hell does the color of his couch have to do with anything?" Trumble asked, looking at Handy like he had a screw loose.

"I have a feeling I might know this couch. What's his number? I'll call him back and ask him."

"I've got a better idea," Trumble said. "Here's his address," he said holding up a piece of paper. "You can go pick up this finger and check out the couch for yourself."

Handy jumped out of his chair, ran over and grabbed the piece of paper, and headed for the door. "Thanks, Captain. You might have just made my day."

Trumble watched as Handy left the room and frowned. "I think that guy needs a vacation," he muttered.

Fran opened her eyes and stared at the ceiling. She didn't feel well. She had been sleeping on and off all afternoon. She sat up and yawned. Deciding a cup of chicken noodle soup would taste good, she stood up and started to walk to the kitchen. She hesitated for a moment when the doorbell rang. She walked the rest of the way into the kitchen and stood by the sink, waiting for the person to leave.

The bell rang again, followed by a couple of knocks. Suddenly, feeling sick to her stomach, she put her head over the sink and threw up.

"She's never home," the young teenager told his friend. "I'm going to stop delivering the paper if she doesn't pay me."

"Why don't you leave her a note?" his friend asked. "That's what I would do."

"Good idea. Let's go back to my house and write it. We can bring it back later."

The two boys jumped on their bikes and rode off.

"Just look at that thing," Mike Myers said loudly. "My kid could have lost an eye."

"Where exactly was this," Detective Handy asked, taking the napkin from Myers and opening it.

"Show him, Janice."

Janice pointed to the spot on the couch. "Here," she told him. "Near as we can tell it was stuck behind this cushion. It must have been pretty far down because when Mike brought the furniture home, I cleaned it really good and I never noticed it. When the boys started jumping up and down, it must have moved up a little and when Perry fell, he landed right on top of it."

"You said when Mike brought it home. I gather you bought this second-hand and recently," Handy said, looking at the couch and chair "Is that right?"

"That's right," Mike replied. "Paid good money for it, too. They don't make furniture like this anymore. I didn't even hesitate to buy it when I saw it. Good, solid set. The lady who sold it was okay, but she's in for one hell of a lawsuit, I can tell you."

"Was the lady's last name Figg?" Handy asked.

Mike looked surprised. "How do you know that?"

"I've seen this furniture before," Handy said.

"Well, as they say, it's a small world," Mike declared.

"That it is. By the way, how is your little boy?"

"He'll be fine. He'll probably have a scar on his cheek for the rest of his life, though," Janice answered.

"Like hell, he will. That Figg lady is going to pay for his doctor bills and that includes plastic surgery if he needs it."

"Do you know who the finger belongs to, Detective?" Janice asked.

"I can't say for sure, but we'll run some tests when I get it back to the lab. They've come a long way with DNA testing, so if we're lucky we'll get a hit and find out who it belonged to."

"It didn't smell, you know," Janice blurted out.

"Excuse me?" Handy said.

"The finger didn't smell. It's mostly bone anyway and part of it is missing. If there had been a lot of tissue and skin on it - well, I think it would have smelled. Don't you agree, Detective?"

"Most likely. Are you sure you'll be able to keep your boys off of the couch until forensics are through doing their job?"

"I personally guarantee that no one will touch that couch, Detective," Mike said.

"And, once your men are done with it, it's going in the garbage," Janice declared.

"Like hell, it is," Mike said loudly. "I paid good money for that furniture and I'm not tossing it out just because we found one little finger in it."

"Mike!" Janice exclaimed.

"I mean it. We'll get some professional cleaners in here and make sure it's nice and clean. I'm willing to pay for that, Janice. But, the couch stays."

CHAPTER TWENTY-FOUR

Thursday, December 16th

Fran decided she should eat a piece of toast and drink a cup of tea. She knew she needed to get something in her stomach, even though the odds were that she'd throw it up. She felt her forehead, trying to see if she was still running a fever. It felt cool and she realized that her body didn't feel so hot anymore either. *Maybe whatever I had is gone,* she thought. *It was probably just a two-day flu thing.* She jumped when her piece of toast popped up out of the toaster. *I'm like a nervous cat.* She smiled as she thought about Sammy. *I miss him. Maybe I should get a kitten. At least I'd have some company here in this big house. I can't believe it's only been ten days since Pheebs died. It seems like she's been gone for months already. At least no one's come knocking on my door asking a bunch of stupid questions.*

Fran buttered her toast and sat down at the table. As she was about to take a bite, the doorbell rang. "What the hell!" she exclaimed. "If that's the damned paperboy again, I'll..."

She walked into the living room and swung open the door. "What?" she shouted and immediately took a step back. "I'm sorry, I thought it was someone else."

"Are you okay, Ms. Figg?" Detective Handy asked. "You don't look so good."

"No, I'm not okay. I have the flu," she whined. "I suggest you keep your distance unless you want to catch it."

"I'll risk it. I need to talk to you."

"Detective, I'm not up to having a conversation with you. Can't you come back in a couple of days?"

"I'm afraid not," Handy replied, pushing the door open all the way. He walked into the living room. "Shall we sit?"

Fran glared at him. "I'd like you to leave."

"I'm afraid I can't do that. I'd like you to sit down, Ms. Figg."

Fran didn't move. "I want the name of your superior officer."

"It's Captain Trumbler." Detective Handy sat down on the overstuffed chair and took out his little black notebook. "Do you remember the name of the man that your sister sold your old couch and chair to?"

Fran walked over to the couch and sat down.

"Ms. Figg? Would you answer my question?"

"I have no idea. I didn't know she was going to sell it until after the fact. I never asked her what his name was."

"It was Mike – Mike Myers and his little boy got injured a couple of days ago from something that was stuck in the back of that couch."

Fran stared at him.

"Do you know what it was?" Handy asked her.

"I'm sorry, but I don't feel like playing guessing games with you. I'm afraid I have no idea what you're talking about. I'm running a fever and I need to go lie down."

"We found a finger. Well, it wasn't the whole finger. Part of it was missing. It seems it had been there for a while. Can you imagine that? A man buys a couch and then finds out that there's a finger stuck in it. That had to be a shock, don't you think?"

Fran closed her eyes, trying to stay in control of her emotions. She opened them and looked at Handy. "I guess."

"Better still, Ms. Figg, we've matched that finger to a person." He looked at her, waiting for some type of response. Nothing. "Aren't you even a little curious?" he finally asked her.

"Not really. Detective, I need to go lie down."

"Pastor Swinger. The finger matches his DNA. We can't figure out how his finger wound up in your old couch. Perhaps, you'd like to enlighten me."

Fran shook her head. "I haven't a clue. If - and that's a big if – if it really is his finger..." She shrugged. "I don't know. I certainly didn't put it there. I can tell you right now, Detective, that I did not put his finger there," she said, raising her voice. "Maybe it was my sister who did it. Unfortunately, we can't ask her, can we?"

"I'm sorry about her accident. No one deserves to die like that."

Fran looked away. "She was a good person."

"How much do you know about the day that Pastor Swinger was here?"

"Just what Phoebe told me," she answered. "He was here for about fifteen minutes. During that time, he asked if we were doing okay, ate some cookies, and left. That's what I know. That's all I know."

"Do you think Pastor Swinger is dead?"

"I have no idea and frankly, right now, I don't care one way or the other. I'm sick. Besides, you're the detective. You figure it out."

"It would be unusual to find a finger under these circumstances and find out that the person the finger belongs to is still living. I believe that Pastor Swinger is dead, Ms. Figg, and I think you know exactly where the body is."

Fran stared at him for a moment and then broke into a laugh. "You couldn't be more wrong. I don't know what you think you're pulling with this finger story, but I know that your finger – if there even is a finger – didn't come from this house. If you think we cut his finger off – well, prove it. Now, if there's nothing else, I'd like you to leave."

"Are you saying it was you and your sister who did it?"

"I didn't say any such thing," Fran replied, looking confused. "Quit putting words in my mouth."

"You said we, not I. So, it was the two of you?"

"You need to get your hearing checked, Detective. Now, will you just leave?" Fran asked, totally aggravated now and fighting not to lose her temper.

Handy stood up and smiled unpleasantly. "It came from here, Ms. Figg. I know it and I will prove it."

"Fine, you do that." She nodded toward the door. "Don't let the door hit you..." She frowned. "Just leave."

Fran closed and locked the door and went back into the kitchen. "He has no proof," she muttered. She reached into the cupboard and took out a bottle of Jim Beam. She stared at it, debating if she should or shouldn't have a drink.

"Oh, screw it all," she shouted, as she reached for a glass and poured herself a drink. She picked up the glass and waved it in the air. "Here's to you, Pheebs," she exclaimed." She took a big swallow and held the glass up to the light, gazing at the amber liquid. "Here's to you, little sister," she repeated as the tears ran down her cheeks.

CHAPTER TWENTY-FIVE

Friday, December 17th

"Well, Pete, did you find anything interesting?" Detective Handy asked the forensic mechanic.

"There's no doubt that the two front brake lines were cut. The thing is, they weren't cut all the way through, meaning that the car's brakes would have worked for a short time. Regardless, the red warning light would have been on, so the driver would have been aware that there was a problem."

"I don't understand why she would have been driving with the red light on. Phoebe Figg took excellent care of her car. I've checked with her mechanic. She took her car in every six months for service."

"Let me check something else," Pete said.

Handy glanced over at the coffee pot. "That fresh?"

"Help yourself." Pete opened the hood of Phoebe's car and looked around. He moved a few wires out of the way and exclaimed, "Well, this answers that question."

"What's that?" Handy asked, walking back to the car holding a cup of coffee.

"The wire for the warning light has been cut, too."

"Are you sure it was cut and didn't break?"

"It was definitely cut. See here?" Pete held up the two ends of the wire so Handy could take a look."

"Pete, would the average woman know how to do this?"

"What? Cut a few wires? I think so. You can find out how to do almost anything these days by looking it up on the internet. Yeah, I'd say a woman could do it."

"Thanks, Pete."

"No sweat. You think a woman did this?" Pete asked.

"I'm almost positive."

There were six of them standing on the steps and a small porch. Fran looked out of the window and stepped back out of sight. She turned, wondering where to run to avoid them.

"Answer the door, Ms. Figg. I know you're in there. I saw you at the window."

Fran didn't move.

"I have a search warrant. If you don't open the door, we will be forced to break the door down," Handy yelled. He waited a few seconds. "All right, guys, do it."

Fran stepped over to the door and opened it. "What do you want now?"

Handy flashed a paper at her. "We're here to execute this search warrant," he said as he handed her the paper.

"I don't understand. What are you looking for?" she asked innocently.

Handy grinned. "Oh, I'm pretty sure you know, Ms. Figg."

"Well, I don't. Perhaps, if you tell me, I can help you."

"You can help me by sitting on that couch and staying there until we are finished." He turned to the policemen still waiting outside and motioned for them to come inside. "Let's go," he yelled.

"Help yourself," Fran said smugly. "You can take all day if you want, but you're not going to find anything."

"Pretty sure, are you?"

"Of course. There's nothing to find."

"You three take the upstairs," Handy instructed, pointing at three of the policemen. "You two - you're down here with me."

Fran walked over to the couch and sat down. She picked up a magazine and started leafing through the pages. *There's absolutely no way they are going to find anything*, she thought. *No way in hell.*

"There's nothing here," one of the cops told Handy an hour later. "We've used the UV light on every crack and cranny. Nothing has shown up."

"Damn," Handy muttered. "There has to be something."

"Maybe they'll find something upstairs."

"They're about done up there," Handy told the cop.

Fran looked over at the two cops talking and smiled. "Are you okay, Detective? You don't look happy."

Handy ignored her remark, walked by her without a glance, and went upstairs. "How you doing in here?" he asked the cop in the bathroom.

"This is the cleanest bathroom I've ever examined. Even the drains are spotless. If there was any blood in here, it looks like they got it all. I'm through in here."

Handy walked down the hallway and checked with the remaining policemen. "Anything?"

151

"Nope," one of them told him. "It looks like the carpets have been cleaned recently. But, there's no evidence of blood anywhere."

"Shit." He thought for a moment. "Did you check the walls and ceilings yet?"

"Done."

"What about the light fixtures?"

"Detective, we've gone over everything. There just isn't anything here."

Handy stood in a bedroom doorway and glanced down the hall. His eyes settled on the top of the bathroom door. "Get me something to stand on," he said.

"Like what?"

"A stool or chair. Anything. Just get it."

The cop looked around the bedroom, noticed a small ottoman by a chair, and grabbed it. "Will this do?"

"Perfect." Handy took the stool and placed it close to the bathroom door. He stepped onto it and grinned. "Give me an evidence bag," he said, as he gloved up.

"What is it?" one of the cops asked.

"We'll see." He gently rubbed his finger along the top of the door, allowing a few small particles to fall into the bag. He stepped down. "Use the UV light up here." He waited while the cop ran the light over the area. "Well?"

"They're small. I mean really small. But we definitely have a couple of drops of blood. I'll swab them."

"Yes!" Handy exclaimed softly. "We got her now." He handed the bag with the small particles to one of the forensic men. "Get this checked out. I need to know as fast as possible."

"You know this is going to take a day or two?" the man informed him.

"Put a rush on it." Handy walked out of the bathroom and into the hallway. "Okay, men, I guess that's it then," he said loudly." He walked down the stairs. "We're done here," he told Fran.

"I told you that you wouldn't find anything," she said sarcastically. "What a waste of the citizens' time and money."

"We have to cover all the bases. I'm sorry if this was an inconvenience to you."

"I hope this is the end to all this foolishness, Detective."

"One thing, Ms. Figg."

"What is that?" she asked.

"You have the cleanest drains we've ever examined."

Fran glared at him. "Just take your men and get out of here. I'm sick of your shit."

Handy grinned and turned to the other policemen. "Good job, guys. Let's go."

CHAPTER TWENTY-SIX

Monday, December 20th

Captain Trumble looked across the table at Handy. "You're positively sure you have enough for an arrest warrant?"

"The only way we could have more is if she confessed. We have Swinger's finger, which was found in her couch, we..."

"But the couch wasn't found in her possession, so a good defense attorney could get that thrown out."

"Possibly, but we also found Swinger's blood on the door in her bathroom plus two small chips of bone that came from him. Those were also in her bathroom."

"You're sure it's his?"

"Without a doubt."

"That still doesn't prove that she killed him."

"Don't forget our eyewitness." Handy reminded him, smiling.

"Ah, yes. That should seal the deal. I'll call the D.A. and get an arrest warrant. Do you think we should go for first-degree murder?"

"For starters. Absolutely." Handy replied.

Are you ready to move on this?"

"I'm ready as soon as you say go."

Fran sat at the kitchen table, enjoying her second cup of coffee. She was feeling much better than she had a few days ago and she had decided to use some long overdue vacation time. Right now, a sandy beach and warm temperatures were sounding good. She looked at the brochure she had picked up at a local travel agency and smiled. Aruba, it is, she decided and drew a big circle around the resort where she planned to stay. Looking at the calendar hanging on the wall, she wondered if it was too late to book a trip leaving before Christmas. That didn't give her much time to get ready.

"Why not?" she mumbled. "Nothing is keeping me here." She stared at the calendar for a moment, then sat back, and fought back the tears. She had almost forgotten that Phoebe's birthday was tomorrow. She regretted how Phoebe had died. It had to be terrible to burn to death. She missed her more than she imagined she would.

Oh, well. What's done is done, she thought. *"I can't change it now.* She picked up the phone and called the agency, crossing her fingers that there was an available room at the resort.

At five-thirty-six on the afternoon of December 20th, Fran Figg was arrested for the murder of Pastor Swinger. It was not a pretty sight, as she did not go easy. It took four strong policemen to carry her out of her house and deposit her into the back of Detective Handy's squad car.

The neighbors covered their children's ears to keep them from hearing her foul language, as she was carried to the car. One woman was overheard asking her neighbor what 'that word' meant. There was not an official in the entire police department who did not have their lives threatened and promises of their balls being fed to the dogs. No, she did not go easy.

Detective Handy stood outside of his police vehicle, listening to her screaming threats, and decided he preferred a quiet trip to the station. He motioned to a uniformed officer to come over to him.

"Yes, Sir," the officer said.

"I want you to drive my car to the station."

The officer glanced up at him and then down at his feet. "I prefer not to, Sir."

"I wasn't giving you a choice, Officer."

"No, Sir, you weren't. But I still prefer not to."

"Oh, for God's sake." Handy walked over to the group of officers standing around outside of the Figg house. "Which one of you had the brilliant idea to put that woman in my car?" he yelled.

One by one, the men looked either down at their shoes or up at the sky.

"I want an answer. Now!" Handy shouted.

"It was me, Sir," a soft voice confessed.

Handy looked at the female officer and grimaced. "Shit," he mumbled under his breath. He pointed at her. 'You. You're with me."

"Me, Sir?"

"Come on. We're taking that screaming banshee to the station."

"You want me to come with you, Sir?"

"You're riding shotgun." He glanced at her, thinking that she was extremely good-looking. "What's your name, officer?"

"Officer Swallows, Sir. Mia Swallows."

Detective Handy looked away, fighting with every muscle in his body not to laugh.

"It's all right, Sir," Officer Swallows said, noting his reluctance to look at her. "You aren't the first person to laugh."

Handy grinned. "Man, your parents didn't do you any favors, did they?"

"It's my married name, Sir. I should have continued using my maiden name. However, my husband didn't like that idea."

"Well, you could always hyphenate your last names."

"That would make it even worse."

"Really? What's your given name?" Handy asked her.

"Gladly."

Handy stared at her. "No way!" he exclaimed as he walked away from the car, laughing so hard he was almost doubled over.

"What the fuck's so funny, you asshole?" Fran screamed from the back seat, as she watched Handy through the window.

Handy turned and looked at Officer Swallows. 'I am so sorry, Officer. That was so unprofessional of..." His body started shaking with laughter and he turned away. "You have got to change your name," he said, not able to look at her.

"My husband won't consider it," she said, grinning. "Doesn't matter anyway. We're not getting along. I think we may get divorced. I'll happily go back to Gladly if that happens."

Handy took a couple of deep breaths and tried to get himself under control. "I really am sorry," he told the officer. "Perhaps it would be better if you didn't ride with me."

"Oh, that's okay, Sir. I'd consider it an honor to ride with you." She opened up the door and sat down in the passenger seat.

Handy hesitated, opened his car door, and got in. He turned and looked at Fran in the back seat. "Not one word. Do you understand?"

She stuck her tongue out at him. "You can't keep me quiet."

"Here's the thing, Ms. Figg. I can." He glanced over at Swallows. "Show her what we keep in our glove compartments, Officer."

Officer Swallows reached into the vehicle's glove compartment and took out a muzzle. She glanced over at Handy, who nodded yes. She held it up for Fran to see.

"You can't put that on me," Fran said, obviously terrified and unsure if he could or not.

"You open your mouth one more time and you'll find out. Now sit back and be quiet."

"You wouldn't!" Fran yelled.

Handy reached for the muzzle. "Officer, would you assist me?"

"All right," Fran yelled. "I'll be quiet."

"Excellent choice," Handy said smiling. He put the car into drive and headed for the police station.

"Thanks for your assistance, Officer," Handy told Swallows.

"My pleasure, Sir,' she replied as she turned to leave the room.

"Officer Swallows," he called to her.

Yes, Sir?" she asked.

"Again, my apologies."

She grinned. "No problem. Thank you."

Handy smiled as he watched her walk away. He felt good. He did not doubt that Fran Figg had killed Swinger, that a jury would find her guilty, and that she would go to jail. He knew there would be further charges, but right now all he wanted was to go home, kick off his shoes, and see his family. And, share a laugh with his wife when he told her about Officer Swallows.

CHAPTER TWENTY-SEVEN

<u>Tuesday, December 21st</u>

Fran glanced around the conference room. She turned to the police matron, who was escorting her. "Do you know where my lawyer is?"

"I'm sorry, ma'am. I have no idea."

District Attorney John Atti followed Detective Handy and Captain Trumble into the room and took a seat by the far wall. He watched as Handy and Trumble sat down at the table and acknowledged Fran.

"It seems your attorney is running late," Handy commented.

"I have nothing to say until he gets here," Fran said bluntly. "So don't even think about asking me any questions."

"We'll give him five more minutes," Trumble told her. "If he's not here by then, we're leaving and you are going back to your cell."

Fran stared at him.

"Ah, here's your guy now," Handy told her, as a smartly dressed, clean-shaven man with gorgeous white hair stepped into the room.

160

"Fran, how you doing?" he asked. "Gentlemen, good to see you. Sorry, I'm late. You never know what the traffic is going to be like," he told them.

"Good to see you, too, Tony," Handy replied.

Anthony Bracchi set a stack of folders down on the table and took a seat next to Fran. "Shall we start?"

Trumble sat back in his chair. "Detective Handy, why don't you begin?" He reached over and started the tape recorder.

Handy went through the usual - stating the date, the time, who was present at the meeting, and ended with reading Fran her rights. "I know you were Mirandized when you were arrested, Ms. Figg. I have repeated it so that there is no question, in the future, that this procedure was done. Also, I'm not completely sure if you remember that I did this yesterday considering the excitable state you were in." He cleared his throat, reached over, picked up a glass of water, and took a sip.

"I remember," Fran told him.

"Before we get into the indisputable evidence we have showing that you killed Pastor Swinger, I would like to give you a chance to make a statement. We'd like to hear your side of the story."

Fran glanced at her attorney, then back at Handy. "You can't have any evidence." She looked at her attorney again. "I didn't do anything. Will you please do your thing and get me out of here?"

"I'm afraid it isn't quite that simple," he told her. "Bail will be discussed at your arraignment."

"When's that?" Fran asked.

"Either later today or tomorrow morning." He looked at Handy. "Sorry. Please, continue."

"Would you care to make a statement?" Handy asked her again.

"My client has nothing to say at this time," Bracchi told Handy.

"The hell I don't," Fran yelled. "This is all a crock of bullshit and you know it, Detective."

"Please, Ms. Figg. If you have nothing constructive to say…" Handy looked at her. "Please, let me continue."

"Tell me what you've got," Bracchi said. "Let me know what you're working with."

"It's not good, Tony."

Bracchi smiled. "I don't expect it to be. I'm sitting here with all the big guns. You've got your boss here and the D.A. over there waiting to make a deal if she confesses. I'm not expecting good."

Fran looked shocked. "Confesses. When hell freezes over!"

Ignoring her outburst, Handy opened up a folder and picked up the first sheet of paper. "As you know, disclosure isn't mandatory in this state. However, I'm going to give you most of the stuff we have so far. With this evidence, I'm hoping you can get your client to confess. If she will, the D.A. is willing to cut a deal to avoid a jury trial."

"Okay," Bracchi said, sighing. "Let me have it."

"We have determined that sometime during the day on October 31st, which was Halloween, your client murdered Pastor Swinger. Although his entire body hasn't been found, we do have one of his fingers, which was found in a couch owned by Ms. Figg. Based on this, we have concluded that she cut him up and disposed of his body in some unknown place."

"Not true," Fran exclaimed. "And, I don't own that couch."

Handy took another sip of water and continued. "After this finger was discovered, a search warrant was issued allowing us to search Ms. Figg's home. During that time, blood was found on a bathroom door. We also found small chips of bone. The blood and the bone have been identified as belonging to Pastor Swinger. We believe that these chips could only have landed on top of the door if a power saw had been used to cut up his body."

Fran rolled her eyes and sighed. "This is so much crap."

"Please, Fran, just listen. Don't talk," Bracchi said.

"Did you hear what he's got?" she exclaimed. "A finger found in someone else's house, some blood, some chips of bone, and what else? Nothing. Is he forgetting that my sister lived there, too? Maybe it was her that did all this shit. I sure know it wasn't me. There's no proof here, Tony. They've got squat."

"Is that correct, Detective? Is that all you have?"

"Of course not. We also have a witness who can verify everything I've told you."

"Huh! That old bag across the street? Some witness she is?" Fran said, grinning.

"Detective Handy, who is she referring to?" Bracchi asked.

"Your client is referring to a woman who lives across the street from her. She has nothing to do with this case."

"Then who's the witness?" Fran asked.

Ignoring her question, Handy continued. "We also have proof that she cut the brake lines on her sister's car, hoping her sister would have a fatal car accident. Phoebe

Figg wanted to sell the house the two sisters own and move on with her life. Fran Figg was against this sale. She rigged the brakes, hoping her sister would be killed in an accident. If her sister, Phoebe died, she would not have to sell or split the proceeds from the sale of the house with her. We are considering the additional charge of attempted murder at this time."

Bracchi raised his head and looked Handy in the eyes. "Attempted? Phoebe Figg isn't dead?"

"She is not."

Fran's head shot up and she stared at Handy. "You're lying," she screamed, as she jumped out of her chair and reached across the table for Handy. The matron, who was standing against the wall behind her, moved quickly and grabbed her, pulling her back from the table. She took the cuffs off her belt, put Fran's arms behind her back, and cuffed her.

The police matron looked at Captain Trumble. "What do you want me to do with her?"

"Sit her back down in that chair," Trumble told her. "We're far from done."

"I'd like a ten-minute break," Tony Bracchi requested. "My client needs to pull herself together."

Handy glanced over at Captain Trumbler who shook his head in agreement. "That sounds like a good idea," Trumbler said. He stood up. "Ten minutes everyone." He turned and walked out of the room.

Detective Handy looked at the district attorney. "John, would you like to get a cup of coffee?"

Atti stood up and stretched. "Sounds good."

The two men exited the room, leaving Fran with her attorney and the police matron. "I'd like a few moments alone with my client," Bracchi told the matron. She hesitated, then left the room.

"You have got to learn to control yourself, Fran," Bracchi told her in a fierce, but low voice. "Your temper isn't helping you here."

"There's no way that Phoebe is alive," Fran said. "I saw the picture of her car in the paper. No one could have survived that."

"Well, obviously, she did and she's talking. You might want to try to cut a deal, Fran. This is not looking good for you."

"I'm not cutting a deal It's still her word against mine," Fran told him. "She was with me every step of the way. If she is going to point a finger at me, I'm going to point it right back."

Bracchi studied her while she spoke, wondering if Phoebe was as guilty of Swinger's death as Fran was. "You killed Swinger, Fran. Are you saying that she helped?"

"I saved her from that fat fuck. His pants were down and he was ready to give it to her. If I hadn't stuck that knitting needle in his ear, he would have raped her."

"But you killed him. Right? She had nothing to do with the murder part?"

"Maybe she didn't, but she sure helped me cut him up and throw him away. She's as guilty as I am."

"The point here, Fran, is that you should have called the police."

Fran shrugged. "Maybe so. Anyway, they can't convict you for saving your sister from being raped, can they?"

"I think they just might, depending on the jury." He hesitated for a moment. "Fran, I want you to think real hard now. What else could Phoebe have told them? We know about the finger. That probably won't come into play. But, is there anything else? What about the brakes on her car?"

"Seriously, Tony? Do you think I'd try to kill my sister just because she wanted her share of the house? I did not touch those brakes. If they failed, it wasn't my doing?" She stood up and started to pace. "I don't get it," she stated. "If Phoebe wasn't killed in that accident, where has she been all this time?"

"I think that's something we need to find out," Bracchi said. He turned and looked at the door as it opened and the three men walked in. "And, I think it will be very soon." He patted Fran's hand. "Just stay cool."

CHAPTER TWENTY-EIGHT

"I want to know more about Phoebe's accident," Attorney Tony Bracchi said, as everyone settled into their chairs. "We've been under the impression that she was killed in a car accident."

"That is the impression we intended to give," Captain Trumbler said.

"I saw the picture of her car in the paper," Fran exclaimed. "There was nothing left of it. She couldn't have lived through that."

Trumble looked over at Detective Handy. "Do you want to field this one, Detective?"

"I'd be glad to," Handy replied, as he reached into the folder in front of him and pulled out two pictures. He laid them in front of Fran and Bracchi. "This is a picture of Phoebe's car. As you can see, it is in reasonably good condition considering that it hit the car in front of it when the brakes didn't work. We estimate that she was driving about forty-five to fifty miles an hour when the impact took place. Now, this is a picture of a car that was in an accident and exploded," he said pointing to the second picture. "You can see that there is little left of it except the frame. This is the picture that was in the paper."

"That's not Phoebe's car?" Bracchi asked.

"No, it is not. It isn't even the same make."

167

"But..."

Bracchi held up his hand, indicating that Fran should be quiet.

"Was she hurt?"

"Oh, yes," Handy told him. "She had some pretty bad injuries. It was touch and go there for a while."

"But, why the deception? Why fake her death?"

"Phoebe was conscious and talking for a short time after the accident. She blamed Fran and told the police to check out the brakes on her car. I heard about it and decided to use it to our benefit."

"So, you made up the story for the newspapers," Bracchi stated, shaking his head.

"Where is she?" Fran asked in a soft voice. "Can I see her?"

Handy grinned. "In your dreams. She doesn't want to see you."

"I need to talk to her. I didn't mess with her brakes," Fran protested. "Please, you've got to believe me."

"Her car has been examined, Ms. Figg. Will you explain why we found your fingerprints underneath the car? Of course, you won't. You most certainly did cut those brake lines. You wanted your sister dead and you hoped this would be the way to do it."

"I didn't," Fran cried out, rubbing the tears away as they rolled down her cheeks.

Handy pushed a box of tissues across the table to Fran. She pulled a couple out of the box and wiped away her tears.

"Exactly what are the charges against my client?" Bracchi asked.

Detective Handy glanced back at District Attorney Atti. "Sir?"

Atti sat forward in his chair. "The first charge is for the mutilation and illegal disposal of Pastor Swinger's body. Phoebe Figg has confirmed that Pastor Swinger was about to rape her when her sister killed him. Although we do feel that killing him was extreme, we also understand that Fran was not thinking clearly at the moment and just wanted to save her sister. Therefore, we are not charging her with his death. However, If Ms. Figg is found guilty of the first charge, she could be sentenced up to seven years."

Fran reached over and grabbed Bracchi's arm and squeezed it. "That can't be right," she whined.

Atti looked down at the paper he was holding. "The second charge is the attempted murder of Ms. Phoebe Figg. This is a Class X felony and, if found guilty, she could be looking at twenty years in prison."

Fran put her hands over her face and sobbed.

"That's a little rough, don't you think?" Bracchi asked Atti.

"We decided to throw out the first attempt on Phoebe's life. I think we're being generous with these two charges, Tony.

Fran's head jerked up. "What first attempt?"

"When you tried to kill her with that leaded glass you threw at her, hitting her in the head."

"That was a fucking accident, you ass!"

"Mr. Bracchi, do you think you can control your client or should we continue without her?"

Bracchi looked at Fran. "Well? Do you want to be taken out of the room or will you keep your mouth shut?"

Fran put her lips together and pulled her fingers across her mouth. "Zip."

Bracchi grinned. "There's no way I'm going to ask for a deal, gentlemen," Bracchi said. "You haven't got a leg to stand on. All this is circumstantial or hearsay. You have no proof that Fran did any of these things, except the word of her sister. It looks like a she said/she said situation. If you decide to go to trial, I'll have all this crap thrown out before the judge even starts jury selection."

"Excuse me," the district attorney interrupted. "I haven't finished." He waited until he got the attention of everyone at the table. "Thank you. The third charge is murder in the first degree."

"What?" Fran yelled.

"What are you talking about?" Bracchi asked loudly. "Who did she kill?"

The D.A. glanced at Detective Handy. "Detective?" he asked.

Handy looked at Fran, trying not to smile. "Fran Figg, you are under arrest for the murder of Gary P. Santoni. You have the right to remain silent. Anything you say can and will be used against you in a court of law. You have the right to an attorney. If you cannot afford an attorney, one will be provided for you. Do you understand the rights I have just read to you? With these... "

"Will you all just shut up?" Fran interrupted. She put her head down on the table and closed her eyes.

"Who the hell is Gary P. Santoni?" Bracchi shouted.

EPILOGUE

One Year Later

CHRISTMAS DAY

December 25th

Phoebe looked around the visitor's room. She spotted Fran sitting at a round table in the back and took a deep breath to steady her nerves. She had not seen her sister since the trial and she was surprised at how much Fran had aged.

Holding a large shopping bag in one hand and her cane in the other, Phoebe limped over to the table and smiled. "Is it okay if I sit down?"

"Fran glanced up at her and shrugged. "Do what you want." She stared at Phoebe. "Still skinny, I see. How long do you have to use that?" she asked, motioning to the cane Phoebe was using.

Phoebe set the large shopping bag down on the floor and pulled out a chair. "It all depends on how my physical therapy goes. It could be a few more months or I might need it forever," she replied as she sat down. "I take it one day at a time."

"Yeah, well, shit happens."

"Thanks to you."

Fran didn't say anything.

"Sorry, I shouldn't have said that. How are they treating you in here? Do you need anything?"

Fran stared at her. "I need to get the fuck out of here. Is there anything you can do about that?" she asked sarcastically.

"Please, Fran, don't start."

"Why did you tell them about Gary, Pheebs? I wouldn't be in here if you had kept your mouth shut. We could have gone the rest of our lives and no one would have known."

"I had to tell them everything to get immunity. If they ever found out that you killed Gary and I helped you cover it up... Well, I could be prosecuted. I couldn't take a chance on that happening, so I told them everything."

"That's my Pheebs. Always looking out for number one and to hell with everyone else," Fran said, raising her voice.

"That's not fair, Fran. Why should I go to jail for helping you? Besides, you were probably going to jail anyway."

"I might have for a little while. Or, maybe, not at all. My attorney thinks he would have gotten me off those first two charges. But you put the nail in my coffin and now I'll never get out of here."

"I'm sorry. You know if we had just called the cops, none of this would have happened."

Fran stared at her and shook her head. "Are you still singing that song? Well, if you hadn't opened the door and let Swinger in, none of this would have happened."

"Please, let's not fight," Phoebe said. She reached into her purse, took out some papers that were folded, and opened them. "I need you to sign these papers, Fran."

"Seriously? That's the reason that you're here? Unfuckingbelievable. I should have known you had an ulterior motive for coming here."

"I came to see you. I've missed you, Fran."

Fran stared at her and smirked. "Yeah, I just bet you have," she said sarcastically."

"I have a buyer for the house and ..."

"That was fast," Fran interrupted.

"No, it wasn't. It's been almost a year since I put it on the market. It hasn't been easy to sell a house where two murders took place."

"Two? You mean one. Swinger wasn't murdered. He was killed when I saved you from being raped, if my memory serves me."

"Sorry. One murder. I need your signature on these papers."

"In your dreams, Phoebe. I told you before that I wasn't selling my house."

"You'll get your share, of course. Your attorney needs to be paid, and there are costs for filing an appeal. Unless you don't want him to appeal. Although, I have talked to him and it seems that all he's waiting for is payment for services already rendered before he'll take your case any further."

"Maybe I should get a different attorney," Fran said smugly.

"Maybe you should. Although, I doubt anyone is going to take you on as a client when you haven't paid for your last attorney." She glanced over at a prison guard and waved.

"What are you doing? Fran asked.

"What is it?" the guard asked as she approached Phoebe.

"I understand you have a pen for us to use. My sister needs to sign some documents."

"What she really means, Val, is that she's afraid I'll poke her eyes out with it and she'd like you to protect her."

"Please, Fran, just sign the papers." Phoebe smiled at Val. "I really appreciate this."

"I really appreciate this," Fran said mocking her sister.

"It's this or you'll never get your appeal, Fran," Phoebe declared.

Fran glared at her. "Oh, to hell with it. Just give me the damn pen."

Val put the pen on the table in front of Fran and stood behind her as Fran signed the documents. She reached for the pen as soon as Fran had signed the last page.

"Happy now?" Fran asked. She glanced up at Val. "I'd like to go back to my cell."

"Thank you, Fran." Phoebe picked up the papers and put them into her purse.

"Eat shit." Fran stood up and turned her back on her.

"Wait," Phoebe called out

Fran turned and looked at her. "What?"

"Merry Christmas."

Fran's mouth dropped open in disbelief as she stared at Phoebe. She shook her head, turned, and started to walk away.

"Fran, wait a minute. I have something for you."

Fran hesitated. "What is it?" she asked, without turning and looking back at her sister.

Phoebe reached into the shopping bag and pulled out a box tied up with a big red Christmas bow. "Look, I baked you some Christmas cookies."

About the Author

I was born in Idaho in 1939. My father's job demanded that we frequently move and, by the age of ten, I had lived in Idaho, Montana, Colorado, Michigan, and Wisconsin.

I am the proud mother of three wonderful sons and two fantastic grandsons. I have no plans to acquire another husband, as they are just too much work.

For most of my life, I worked as an accountant. Two years before I retired, I made a complete switch in careers and managed two Curves fitness facilities in Illinois. I retired in 2002 and moved to Branson, MO. In 2012, I moved to Indiana to be closer to my family and have resided in Highland since then.

I enjoy a good laugh and figure it's my sense of humor that keeps me going when times are tough. Reading has always been one of my passions and I still read a couple of books a week.

In 2014, I wrote my first book, *Blueberries and Bears and My Brother's Shoes*, a book about growing up in the forties and fifties. After I self-published it and gave it to friends and family to read, they encouraged me to get serious about my writing.

I never thought that, at the age of 76, I would become an author. I set a goal for myself to write at least ten books before I die. I've made the ten plus and I'm pretty sure I have a lot more novels kicking around in this head of mine.

I certainly am enjoying my retirement knowing, when I get up each morning, I have something to look forward to. You can find out more about me and my books at www.susanlpare.com. Please visit me there, sign up to be on my readers' list, and feel free to send me your comments.

THE FINGER BY SUSAN L. PARÉ